IT'S 1977, AND BATTLES RAGE ON SAN FRANCISCO BAY OVER ATTEMPTS TO EVICT HUNDREDS OF PEOPLE, MOSTLY YOUNG AND REBELLIOUS, LIVING IN HOUSEBOATS

In the waning days of the hippie movement, along a stretch of San Francisco Bay known as Waldo Point, hundreds of young people live in an improvised community of off-kilter houseboats, taking inspiration from their guru, garrulous eighty-four-year-old Achille Palaiologos.

A change in property ownership threatens the community's existence: the new owner, a developer, wants everyone evicted. The houseboaters fight back, enlisting in their cause Legal Aid attorney Rick Spenser. Battles ensue, both legal and physical, in the courts and on land and water. After a daring act of sabotage upends the developer's plans, the houseboaters split into bitterly opposed factions over whether or not to propose a compromise plan. Meanwhile Rick, though supposedly committed to girlfriend Tiffany Wong, is attracted to houseboat leader Becky Yates. Both these conflicts culminate in a day and night of tragedy, betrayal and fear.

In the aftermath, Rick strives to repair his relationship with Tiffany, while Rick and Becky together struggle to save the community and end the houseboat wars.

"...a fun and thoughtful read...probes the 'nobody's right when everybody's wrong' culture clashes of the 1970s...put on your favorite old vinyl album, read and enjoy the ride."—*Don Daglow, author of The Fog Seller*

"The Sausalito, California houseboat wars of the '70s...makes for a wild chapter in Bay Area history and an entertaining read."—*Cyra McFadden, author of The Serial: A Year in the Life of Marin County*

"...a fascinating, fictional chronicle of...the houseboat community of Sausalito, California...suspenseful and a page turner. I highly recommend this well written book."—*Colleen Rae, author of One Sausalito Summer*

"In this thriller, a houseboat community's legal case against developers in 1977 California culminates in murder...The attorney protagonist getting caught up in more melodrama than lawyering makes for an unusual but convincing tale."—*Kirkus Reviews*

HOUSEBOAT WARS

Charles Bush

Moonshine Cove Publishing, LLC
Abbeville, South Carolina U.S.A.
First Moonshine Cove edition March 2019

ISBN: 978-1-945181-542
Library of Congress PCN: 201934152
Copyright 2019 by Charles Bush

Book cover design by Moonshine Cove Staff, Cover Images public domain

About the Author

Charles Bush is a former attorney whose clients ranged from inmates on San Quentin Prison's Death Row to residents of embattled San Francisco Bay houseboat communities. His first novel, *What Went Wrong With Oscar Toll?* (2014), told the story of a lawyer handling a death penalty appeal and won the award for Best Legal Thriller in the 2015 National Indie Excellence Book Awards. Charles is currently working on a historical novel set in eighteenth-century China. He was born in Kansas City, Missouri; graduated from Harvard College and the University of Chicago Law School; and currently lives in San Francisco with his husband in an 1877 Victorian they've renovated.

Charles' website can be found at www.charlesbush-author.com

To

JANE KOESTEL

and

CALVIN LAU

Preface

This is a work of fiction. Although I was witness
to and participant in the houseboat wars that roiled
the waters of San Francisco Bay during the 1970s
and 80s, this novel does not purport to be an accurate
recounting of those years. Consider it instead a
fantasy, or history refracted by a funhouse mirror

HOUSEBOAT WARS

1
PARKING LOT AND TRUCK

The parking lot lay only footsteps ahead, shrouded in darkness. The sun had long since set, clouds blacked out the stars and moon. There was no overhead lighting — never had been in this converted patch of dirt. No vehicles were coming in or out with their lights on.

In front of me ran a ragged line of cars and trucks, beyond that an aisle, then another ragged line of vehicles. My Mustang was parked in the second line, across the aisle.

Still feeling the effects of the too-many Scotches I'd just drunk, I dragged my feet across the rough dirt surface and eased myself around a parked van. I stepped into the aisle, and just as I did, a large truck located at the end turned on its headlights and illuminated a broad swath of light in front of me.

I halted. How nice. Was the truck driver doing me a favor? Or was it just coincidence he'd provided light exactly when I needed it?

I began to cross the aisle. The big truck roared its engine, lurched forward and *headed straight for me!*

I froze. But only for a split-second; then I ran fast as I could, finally tucking myself into the space between my car and the one next to it. The big truck roared past, spewing dust, gravel, engine noise and hatred.

My heart raced, I started to sweat. What was going on?

There was no way around it. I was under attack. The truck deliberately tried to run me down. It wasn't an accident, or a failure to see me. The truck clearly *aimed* at me.

Meanwhile, the truck was backing up. It passed the front of my car again, this time going the opposite direction, and came to a stop roughly where it had started, about forty feet to my right. The truck then repositioned itself in the aisle so that its headlights pointed squarely at me. It resembled an angry dragon crouched in anticipation, the two headlights its eyes, the clattery engine its growl. I tried to see who the driver of the truck was, but the headlights' glare blacked out everything else.

What to do?

I couldn't think, my brain was white noise. I could barely breathe.

Calm down, I told myself. Start breathing, start thinking.

After about thirty seconds, a coherent thought took form. There was no point standing outside. I had a car. I unlocked the Mustang's door and climbed into the driver's seat.

I slumped over the steering wheel. What a day from hell this had been. Early on, I learned that a client, whom I also considered a good friend, had been murdered. Just in the last hour, I'd betrayed the love of my life. Now, a truck was trying to kill me. What had I done to deserve all this?

But I couldn't waste time feeling sorry for myself. I needed to find a way out of the trap I'd fallen into.

I tried to analyze the situation. The truck seemed to be waiting for me to pull out. When I did, would it try to hit me? It seemed completely irrational. While a big truck might be able to hit a pedestrian and get away with little damage to itself, surely hitting a Mustang at high speed would damage almost any truck. Surely whoever was driving the truck would recognize that.

Or would he?

Or would he even care?

Perhaps I could simply outwait the truck. If I did nothing, didn't even turn on my headlights, perhaps the truck would eventually get bored and go away.

Of course, the downside to this strategy was that it would make me even later, and I was already unpardonably late. Oh Tiffany, dear Tiffany, will you ever forgive me?

I decided it was worth a try. I sat in the driver's seat, resolved to wait patiently and watch the problem go away.

I couldn't do it. I was too tense — sweating, trembling, the acrid smell of truck exhaust in my nostrils, the truck's piercing headlights in my eyes. Five seconds seemed like a minute, five minutes like an hour.

Nor did the truck vanish of its own accord. It remained in the center of the aisle, motor running, headlights glaring, hostility exuding.

Time for Plan B.

The truck was to my right. The way out of the parking lot was to the left. If I pulled out of my space and turned left, the truck, assuming the worst, would come at me from behind. I could try to outrun the truck. But that seemed a risky strategy. The truck could build up speed faster than I could, because it was moving in a straight line, whereas I had to make a left turn. Plus, the truck driver probably knew the parking lot better than I did.

Time for some trickery. I'd noticed earlier, when the truck first barreled forward down the aisle, then backed up, and then moved forward to reposition itself, that it needed considerable time to shift gears between forward and reverse. By contrast, since my Mustang was an automatic, I could shift between the two directions rapidly. Could I take advantage of that pair of facts?

Actually, the question was could I take advantage, given my current condition? I'd felt slightly drunk leaving

Becky's boat; now I felt gripped by fear. At least the fear seemed to have flushed out the alcohol.

I began to creep out of my parking space, left hand on the steering wheel, right hand on the gearshift, ready for instant action. With my left eye I looked to where I was going; with my right, I watched the truck.

Creep, creep, creep —

The truck's engine let out a guttural roar, its tires buzz sawed on gravel and dirt, and the malevolent shape catapulted forward. I yanked the Mustang's gearshift back to reverse and zipped back into my parking space. The truck rushed past me down the aisle, missing the front end of my car by only an arm's length. The truck came to a halt further down the aisle.

The truck was now to my left, facing away. On the one hand, it was blocking my only way out. On the other hand, I was behind the truck; it could no longer attack me without making another move. And I was no longer staring into its headlights.

I felt better. The ball was now in the truck's court. I could revive the wait-it-out strategy.

But I didn't have to wait. The driver gunned the truck's engine again and began to back up. He passed my parking space, still in reverse gear.

As soon as the front of the truck cleared my space, I charged out, turned left, and sped down the aisle toward the exit. In my rearview mirror I saw the truck's headlines recede into the distance, and I knew the driver was, as I'd anticipated, struggling to shift from reverse to forward.

I exited the parking lot and came to Bridgeway. The light was red, but there were no other cars nearby. I shot across. Then, I raced up the access ramp to Highway 101, accelerator pressed to the floor.

Once I felt confident, I'd escaped the parking lot and the evil truck, a question coiled itself around my frazzled brain, my stiff neck, my sore, tense shoulders. It was a really good question.

How had I gotten myself into this mess?

2
INTAKE DAY

It all began on a warm, seemingly routine afternoon in October 1977.

I worked as a staff attorney at Marin Legal Aid, where my duties included handling intake — interviewing new applicants for our free legal services — one or two afternoons a week. I was on intake duty that October day when three individuals walked into our offices.

They were from Waldo Point, a spot along Richardson Bay just north of Sausalito, they told me. They lived on houseboats, as did virtually everyone else at Waldo Point. And they had come on behalf of an organization called Save Our Waterfront — SOW for short.

Why was SOW coming to Legal Aid? Because the houseboat community at Waldo Point was being evicted. For many years, an eccentric landlord had owned Waldo Point. He followed an anything-goes philosophy in managing his property, and the houseboat community grew up under his neglectful watch. Now, under pressure from county authorities worried about health and safety conditions, the eccentric landlord had sold the property. The buyer was a real estate development group out of San Francisco that planned to evict everyone now living at Waldo Point and redevelop the area as a luxury houseboat marina aimed at the high-end market. To add insult to injury, the development group planned to rename the area from Waldo Point to Strawberry Point Harbor.

SOW wanted Legal Aid to bring a lawsuit to stop it all.

I didn't know what to tell the Houseboat Three. They were asking for a large, complicated lawsuit against at least

14

two defendants, one a sophisticated real estate developer that probably commanded enormous financial resources, and the other the County of Marin, which generally won when sued in local court. And to be honest about it, the various houseboat communities along Richardson Bay enjoyed an unsavory reputation. To us outsiders, the name "Waldo Point" conjured a mysterious netherworld.

On the other hand, I couldn't simply say "no." The Houseboat Three estimated there were around 115 boats at Waldo Point, housing roughly 160 people, almost all of them low-income. Marin Legal Aid's sole reason for existence was to provide free legal assistance in civil cases to the low-income residents of Marin County. Were we going to stand aside while 160 of our supposed beneficiaries were evicted?

I told the three I'd have to get back to them. Then I went to see my boss, Sam. When I told him about my meeting with the houseboaters, he laughed and shook his head. "Want to hear about my one experience representing somebody from Waldo Point?"

"Sure."

"It was an eviction case, and the client's name was . . . Sandra something-or-other; I don't remember her last name. Sandra was tall, thin, dark-haired, and if you really want to know, slutty-looking. I don't remember much about the case — other than the fact we lost — but I do remember a couple of things about Sandra.

"First, in her application, she listed income but gave her occupation as 'hitchhiker.' How did she make money as a hitchhiker? I asked — in retrospect, naively.

"'I'm a prostitute,' she answered nonchalantly. 'There's a group of us. We pick up our johns by hitchhiking on the access road to 101 North. So we call ourselves hitchhikers.'

"Then, at her trial, just as our case was definitively crumbling, she leaned over, pulled on the sleeve of my suit coat, and whispered in my ear, 'You don't happen to have any Percodan on you, do you? I'm really having withdrawal.'"

Sam gritted his teeth and again shook his head.

I remained silent a few seconds, to give Sam time to exorcize the memory of Sandra something-or-other. Then I reiterated what *I* regarded as the crucial fact, that roughly 160 low-income Marin County residents were facing eviction.

"I hear you," he said, his brow furrowed.

"Let me propose something. They invited me down to Waldo Point to take a look and see what their community is all about. I could take them up on their offer."

"That sounds like a good idea. At least it's low-budget."

"Okay. Will do."

That was it. That's how my unsuspecting journey to the dark parking lot and the murderous truck began.

3
THE TOUR – GATE 6

Massive, grey and thoroughly rotten, it walled off the seaward side of the Waldo Point parking lot. It was the long side of an enormous wooden boat. Or more accurately, the *remains* of an enormous wooden boat, for although a skeletal paddlewheel still adorned the behemoth's side and a tall black smokestack tottered on top, the poor boat's rectangular hull was so decrepit it was collapsing onto itself, well along the road to becoming simply a 300-foot-long pile of rotting wood.

Mysteriously, the boat rested entirely on dry land. It was not beached — that would imply an ocean lapping at one edge — but instead simply grounded, dry land in all directions. A sign on the boat read *"CHARLES VAN DAMME."*

Welcome to Waldo Point.

I gingerly stepped out of my Mustang onto the parking lot's rough dirt surface. Three individuals were heading my direction — the same Houseboat Three who'd appeared at our offices earlier that week. Since they'd filled out lengthy application forms, I knew quite a bit about each of them.

My eye went immediately to the lone female of the trio, Becky Yates. She was twenty-five — two years younger than me — the secretary of SOW, and by occupation a retail clothing salesgirl. She was also, I couldn't help noticing, quite the fox, with a cascade of long curly blond hair, oval face, flawless complexion, large sensual green eyes, dimpled chin, suntanned arms and legs, and round, firm breasts untethered by bra.

Becky Yates seemed to favor splashy, sexy clothing. When she'd visited our offices earlier in the week, she'd worn a light summer shift that resembled a patchwork quilt — differently patterned squares of colorful cloth arranged haphazardly. Today her dress was fuchsia — an intense, psychedelic fuchsia — with a pattern of small yellow flowers. You would have noticed her from Seattle.

At the opposite end of the pulchritude spectrum stood Hank Foster — fifty-six years old, an auto mechanic by trade, and a member but not an officer of SOW. Gaunt and weathered, he seemed all hollows, with a head long and bony like that of an old horse and a suspicious stare emanating from sunken eyes. His grayish hair extended long and lank to his shoulders, and he wore an aged grey T-shirt and much-dripped-upon jeans.

The third member of the trio — Kevin Cassidy, age twenty-eight, vice-president of SOW — looked much like me. Average height, slender build, light complexion, sandy hair. He wore a collared shirt and clean jeans, and when he'd visited our offices he'd even carried a briefcase.

Kevin Cassidy's one negative was that on his application form he said he was unemployed with zero income. This was normally a red flag for Legal Aid eligibility purposes; when a potential client reported zero income, we were supposed to ask, "If you don't have any income, how do you eat?" But since Kevin was coming in on behalf of a group and not himself, I'd let the matter slide.

Becky, Hank and Kevin greeted me with smiles and handshakes. "Today we're going to start by giving you a tour of Gate 6," said Kevin, who generally acted as spokesperson for the trio. "Then we'll go down to Gate 5, and there you'll meet the president of SOW."

I hadn't met the SOW president yet. I'd been told he was eighty-four years old and had difficulty getting around, but was eager to meet me at Waldo Point.

"Fine," I said. "But first, what's that?" I pointed to the huge, collapsing boat.

Hank stepped forward to answer. "That's the *Charles Van Damme*, an old bay ferryboat."

"Why is it here?"

"Don Arques bought it and moved it here."

Don Arques — Donlon Arques, to use his full name — was the eccentric landlord whose laissez-faire management of Waldo Point had allowed the houseboat community to flourish.

"Why did Arques do that?"

Hank shrugged. "He liked old ferryboats. He bought several of them."

"Did he ever use them for anything?"

"He didn't. But our president, Achille Palaiologos, lives on one of Arques' old ferryboats, the *San Rafael.*"

I pointed at the rotting hulk facing us. "The president of SOW lives on something like *that?*"

"Yup."

This is going to be weird.

My attention returned to the fact the *Charles Van Damme* sat wholly on land, no water in sight. "How did Arques get a boat this big onto dry land?"

"He dug a channel and floated the *Charles Van Damme* in. Then he filled in the channel and all around the boat."

"Why was it so important for him to have the boat here on dry land?"

Again Hank shrugged. "I guess you'd have to ask him."

I continued staring at Arques' dubious achievement. Hank's explanations weren't very satisfying. But then, how *would* you explain a spectacle so bizarre?

"We better get started on our tour," Kevin said, obviously trying to get off the subject of quirky Donlon Arques. "As I was saying, we're going to start by giving you a tour of Gate 6. Then we'll go down to Gate 5 and you'll meet the president of SOW on the *San Rafael.*"

We headed toward the south end of the *Charles Van Damme.* "Those names — Gate 5, Gate 6 — they go back to the old shipyard, right?" I asked as we walked. I was vaguely aware the entire northern Richardson Bay waterfront had been the site of an enormous shipbuilding enterprise during World War II.

"Exactly," said Hank. "It was called Marinship. There were 20,000 people working here at the peak. The whole area was fenced in, and you had to enter through one of the gates. That's where those names — Gate 3, Gate 5, Gate 6 — came from. The shipyard's long gone, but the names of the gates still live on."

Hank seemed to be the group's historian. "How long have you lived here?"

"Since 1942. Thirty-five years. I was one of the workers at Marinship."

"Wow." Turning to Becky and Kevin, I asked, "And how long have each of you lived here?"

Kevin didn't seem pleased by the question. He looked at Becky.

"I came here in 1971, so six years," she said.

"And you?" I said to Kevin.

"I've been here about four years. Shall we get started?"

Quite a difference in seniority, I thought. No wonder Kevin seemed eager to get off the subject. On the other hand, if Kevin was vice president of SOW, he had to be an accepted member of the community.

Circling the south end of the *Charles Van Damme,* we came to a makeshift gate. On top, multi-colored, cartoonish letters on a wooden board spelled out, "NO TOURISTS BEYOND THIS POINT."

"You have a problem with tourists?"

"Do we?" said Becky. "One morning I was just getting out of the shower, and there were these three guys, German tourists, on my boat. On my boat!"

Lucky German tourists.

Beyond the gate the path turned into a downward-sloping bridge three or four weathered planks wide, with no handrails and supported by only a few rickety posts. With trepidation, I stepped onto the bridge, keeping my eyes down to watch my footing.

The bridge connected to a dock floating in water. It also was constructed of much-weathered wood and lacked handrails. I continued to keep my eyes down as I hopped from the bridge to the dock, then adjusted to the bobbing up and down of the dock.

When finally I looked up, I realized I'd fallen through the rabbit hole. All around me were the houseboats of Gate 6.

All principles of order, symmetry, coherence and pattern had been repealed. No line was plumb, no two corners aligned. All shapes imaginable — circles, squares, rectangles, rhomboids, trapezoids, triangles — coexisted cheek to jowl. Concepts from *Snow White and the Seven Dwarves* competed with concepts from Buckminster Fuller. Water lapped, a scent of bacon and eggs wafted, and a one-eared dog trotted along the dock. Shifting from leg to leg to keep my balance on the swaying, floating dock, I tried to form a concept of the whole, but there was no whole, not even a sum of the parts, only a thousand crazy, mismatched pieces.

"Can we stop here for a moment, so I can get my bearings?"

"Sure."

On second look, I realized there was in fact a unifying theme. Wood. The shear woodiness, unpainted woodiness, of the place was astounding. Wooden docks, wooden ramps, wooden boats, wooden decks, wooden walls, wooden shingles, even, in the distance, a wooden totem pole. And with wood came the ills to which wood is subject — weathering, bleaching, rotting, breaking.

I narrowed my focus to a single nearby houseboat. Architecturally, it looked like three wooden boxes perched precariously on top of a rowboat. Or maybe not a rowboat, the vessel looked larger — and very rusty. The three boxes, windowless and arranged in a row, consisted of a taller box in the middle and shorter ones on either side.

The taller box was emblazoned with what looked like a Grateful Dead concert poster — a swirling mass of curlicues, flames and dots centered around a goddess face, all painted in psychedelic shades of pink, orange, purple and blue. The decoration of the two smaller boxes, on the other hand, consisted simply of wide vertical stripes painted in pastel colors — yellow, orange, robin's-egg blue. One side of the vessel bore an inscription in an exotic script I couldn't decipher. Sanskrit? Tibetan? The spears of a yucca plant peaked out on top.

While trying to make sense of the three-box boat, I started to notice the smell of raw sewage in the air. "How do people here get rid of their . . . waste?" I asked.

My three guides looked at each other sheepishly. Finally Becky said, "A few people have composting toilets. Unfortunately, most people just do it in a jar and then open a window and throw it overboard."

I stared at Becky, unsure what to say. She had a low, breathy voice I found extremely sexy. Her golden locks and fuchsia dress glowed in the afternoon sun. Yet she was talking about people tossing their crap into Richardson Bay.

Taking my silence as requiring a fuller answer, Becky continued. "It's terrible. We know it's terrible. And we want to work with the county to get the area sewered and everything cleaned up."

After another pause, Kevin said, "Shall we move on?"

"Sure"

The Gate 6 dock plan was a maze. No dock continued in a straight line for long. Instead, a dock would split, turn right, turn left or simply end. Without a guide, any outsider would be lost.

Running alongside most of the docks were poles supporting a tangle of unruly, exposed wires. "Is that your electrical system?" I asked.

"Electrical and telephone."

I waited for some sort of acknowledgement of the safety issue. None came.

"Doesn't look terribly safe," I said.

"We definitely recognize all the wiring and electrical down here has to be upgraded."

"And we would like to work with the county to do just that," added Becky.

"Have you tried? Have you gone to the county?"

"We have. But they say they've already issued a permit for redevelopment of Waldo Point, and because of that, they can't consider or even talk about any other plan.

"You see, three years ago, the county forced Donlon Arques to submit a plan for redoing the entire Waldo Point area, with regular straight docks extending out into the bay, sewer lines running along the docks, and all the boats tied up to the docks and hooked up to the sewers. A lot of us at Waldo Point were aware of this. But Don assured us the only reason he'd submitted the plan was because the county had forced him to, and as far as building out the plan was concerned, he intended to move very slowly, if at all. He said nobody would be displaced, everybody would be taken care of.

"But now this new group is intending to do just the opposite — build out the plan quickly and displace everybody. And when we talk to the county, they say that in buying the property, the new group, Strawberry Point Harbor Associates, inherited the approvals for the old Arques plan, and therefore the new group has, quote, vested rights, unquote. I'm not sure I understand exactly what vested rights means, but in any event, the county won't even talk to us."

I looked at Becky sympathetically, but said nothing. It was hard to know what to make of the houseboaters' complicated legal situation.

We continued to hop from floating dock to floating dock. At one juncture three young men worked on a carpentry project, apparently a dock extension. The three looked like clones of each other — each shirtless, deeply tanned and muscular, and topped by an oversized shock of frizzy blond hair.

Around another bend in the docks, a teenage girl — long straight yellow hair, clad in a sleeveless white shirtdress — stood on the deck of a boat, smoking a cigarette, a vacant look on her face. Opposite her, a rangy orange cat lay on a railing, soaking up the sun. Rock music sounded faintly in the background. Another dock beyond, a cloud of marijuana smoke overcame even the pervasive odor of raw sewage.

We came to a boat consisting of an L-shaped structure wrapped around a wooden deck. The deck was packed with colorful potted plants and quirky bric-a-brac — a pumpkin, a pair of moose antlers, a carnival mask, a tall pole hoisting wooden disks on which were painted mysterious geometric shapes. The façade of the L-shaped structure was part Japanese-style vertical wood slats, part boards painted turquoise blue, and part multi-paned windows that didn't quite fit. A smokestack popped out of the structure's roof. A large reddish-brown dog lay on the deck, its front paws hanging over the edge. A turquoise-blue rowboat floated by the side. Wind chimes rang softly. Everything seemed cozy, homey.

"That's Becky and Kevin's boat," said Hank.

I felt a jolt. Were Becky and Kevin a couple? Somehow I'd never thought of that possibility.

I looked at the two of them. "Are you two . . . together?"

They sheepishly nodded and mumbled yes.

The news of Becky and Kevin's couplehood threw me off balance. But why?

Was it because I was worried about the credibility of SOW, if half of its leadership came from a single household? Actually, since I hadn't yet met the group's president, it was too early to judge.

Or was it because I'd been attracted to Becky? Had I subconsciously hoped my meeting her might somehow lead to something more?

If so, I needed to clean up my act. In the first place, a male lawyer hitting on a female client was a gross violation of legal ethics.

Even more important, wasn't I supposed to be in love? Tiffany Wong and I met three months earlier, and our relationship had progressed rapidly. We were now both starting to think this might be *it*. I was going to be seeing her in only a few hours. I shouldn't be mooning over someone else.

Becky, Kevin, Hank and I resumed our walk through the Gate 6 maze, heading generally away from land, out toward the middle of Richardson Bay. I noticed, rising high in the distance over a cluster of low houseboats, a bizarre wooden something-or-other. It looked like an African mask, or maybe a blown-up detail of a totem pole. "What's that?"

"That's the Owl," Kevin said. "Chris Roberts' masterpiece."

"What is it? A boat?"

"It's a houseboat."

"Whose masterpiece?"

"Chris Roberts. He was a sculptor and boat builder. He built several boats, or more accurately boat sculptures, around here, but the Owl is definitely the most noticeable."

I could now see that the bizarre something-or-other did somewhat resemble an owl. The narrow-set eyes. The beak. The wide, pointed ears. "Very impressive," I said.

"We love it," said Becky.

The next turn led to a most pleasing sight, a well-built young woman with a smiling face, long curly auburn-colored hair and ruddy sun-kissed skin. Her gypsy-style dress, a vivid mix of reds, oranges and purples, was full of pleats and fabric but left her arms and shoulders bare. She sported a profusion of glittering necklaces and bracelets, so many in fact that when she moved, she jingled.

Becky and Kevin greeted the young woman enthusiastically, and Becky said to me, "Mr. Spenser, we'd like you to meet one of our most loyal members. This is Montse. Montse, this is Mr. Spenser."

"I'm *so* happy to meet you, Mr. Spenser," Montse gushed. "I heard all about the meeting on Tuesday. And after all the good things Becky and Kevin said about you, I couldn't wait to meet you in person."

"Well, I'm flattered. What did you say your name was?"

"Montse. It's short for Montserrat."

"Montse. Okay."

Kevin retook his role as tour guide. "The boats around here are the furthest out into the bay of all the boats at Gate 6. Montse and Ryan, her old man, live in that boat" — he pointed to one at the end of the dock — "and they have a float beside it. We thought we'd take you out to the float, and from there you can see the open bay."

"Great."

We took a ramp from the floating dock to Montse's houseboat, then another ramp from the houseboat to the float. Eventually all five of us were on the float, including Hank, who hadn't said anything in a while. The float rocked and swayed, but eventually settled down.

The view took my breath away. Above, a cerulean sky, unblemished by smog or fog, host to a few small, white puffy clouds. In the distance, the high ridge of the Tiburon Peninsula, patches of green trees alternating with swaths of brown grass. Closer in, sunlight shimmering on the sapphire waters of Richardson Bay.

The loudest sounds were the cries of seagulls and the lapping of waves. A gentle breeze touched the skin. The only snake in this floating Eden was the ever-present smell of human waste.

"Ryan and I love this view," said Montse. "Absolutely love it. And I'm sure you can see why.

"But you know, this view isn't what we like *best* about Waldo Point. What we like best is the sense of community. Here at Waldo Point people help each other. People are always there for each other, through thick and thin. There's no fighting or competing, no backbiting or petty resentments. It's all positive energy, nothing negative. When something needs to be done, people volunteer. Nobody asks for money. People work together, and take joy in what others are doing, and are happy to see other people succeed. I know it sounds corny, but here at Waldo Point, we're like one big happy family."

The magic of the moment and the force of Montse's encomium to houseboat living overwhelmed me. I felt as if I'd seen a vision. What a remarkable community. What a fascinating challenge to the values of mainstream society. And what a tragedy it would be if it were completely wiped out.

But even in my intoxicated state, a small hand of doubt tugged at my mind. Was it really possible? A community of one hundred plus people functioning as one big happy family? With no conflicts, no backbiting, no power struggles, no petty grievances? Montse's description of the Waldo Point houseboat community made it sound like paradise on earth. Did such a thing exist?

The gruff voice of Hank brought us all back to earth. "We'd better get going. Achille's expecting us down at Gate 5."

4
GATE 5 - ACHILLE

We threaded our way back through the Gate 6 maze, walking single-file on the narrow floating docks. Montse joined us; she wanted to be part of the meeting with SOW's president. The jingling of her bracelets and necklaces joined the creaking and sloshing of the docks.

Back on land, we turned south onto a wide dirt road, accompanied by the fragrances of salt, seaweed and sewage. As we walked, Hank positioned himself beside me. "Sir, there's something here I'd like to show you." He unfolded a sheet of paper and handed it to me.

It was a Xerox copy of a page from an 1873 decision of the California Supreme Court. About a third of the way down the page a sentence was underlined in red: "All navigable waters of this State are held subject to a public trust for commerce, navigation and fisheries." About two-thirds down another sentence was underlined: "The right of navigation includes the right of anchorage."

An 1873 California Supreme Court decision didn't mean much by itself. It was now 1977, and any court was going to expect a citation more recent than 1873. After all, in the 104 years since this case had been decided, it could have been overruled, modified, made obsolete by constitutional amendment — any number of things.

On the other hand, Hank's sheet was interesting. It certainly suggested an important research angle should Legal Aid take on the houseboaters' cause.

I looked up at Hank. "Is your area navigable? Does it qualify as navigable waters?"

He nodded. "It's definitely navigable"

I again looked at the sheet. "The right of navigation includes the right of anchorage." Interesting. But I had no idea how much weight this concept could carry.

"I have to be honest with you. I don't know anything about the right of navigation, or what it may or may not include. As you can imagine, in a small legal aid office we don't get too many right-of-navigation cases, and I've never had occasion to research the subject. But I can assure you that if we take on some sort of representation of your group, we'll definitely do that research."

My answer seemed to satisfy Hank, who continued to walk beside me. A few paces later, he said, "I think you'll find our president, Achille Palaiologos, quite a remarkable man. He — "

"Excuse me, but do you think you could go over that name again?"

"A-chille Pa-lai-o-lo-gos."

"Pa-lai-o . . . .?"

"Pa-lai-o-lo-gos. You know, what's interesting about the name is that it's the name of the Byzantine royal family. Achille's actually part of the Byzantine royal family, and a cousin of his is the pretender to the Byzantine throne."

I stopped in my tracks. We were talking about the Byzantine Empire? I was not prepared for this.

"But the Byzantine Empire no longer exists. It hasn't existed for hundreds of years."

"I know, I know. And that's why it's so amazing this family has been able to keep it together over all those years. Most families would have given up."

I pondered this response. Apparently neither Hank nor Achille were the type to give up easily. That might be a red flag in terms of representing SOW. Generally you wanted clients, particularly clients in big cases, to show a *little* flexibility.

When we resumed walking along the dirt road, Hank continued his praise of Achille the Byzantine. "Achille's an amazing person. He's very well educated and has read almost everything under the sun. He's an expert on all the ancient Greek philosophers. He's also known all sorts of famous people, like Alan Watts and Jean Varda."

I recognized Alan Watts' name. His book *The Way of Zen* had been a cult classic when I was in college. I'd never heard of Jean Varda.

"Achille's opinions on things are always so well thought out that you're just amazed anybody can be that intelligent. He's eighty-four years old now, and his eyesight isn't good, but mentally he's still sharp as a tack."

"Did Achille design the Gate 6 dock plan?"

Hank looked puzzled. "No, it sort of designed itself. Why do you ask?"

"I thought it seemed Byzantine."

Hank didn't get the joke, and when I explained it to him, he didn't laugh.

Soon the over-sized and the bizarre reappeared, once again taking the form of a hulking skeleton of a once-great boat, a gray-and-white mass of rotting wood.

This vessel resembled the *Charles Van Damme* I'd seen earlier, but whereas my first view of the Van Damme had been from the side, this boat I was looking at from the front. The front half of the vessel consisted simply of a large, flat, open deck. Back of that, a two-story structure rose up. The bottom story was unenclosed — a void. The upper story was enclosed, with two windows. Taken as a whole, the boat looked like a giant gargoyle sticking out its tongue. The protruding lower deck was the gargoyle's tongue, the first story its mouth, and the upper story its eyes and brow.

31

Not only did this vessel look like a gargoyle, it also sloped. Sloped badly. The right side was significantly higher than the left.

The *Charles Van Damme*, I remembered, had been grounded — surrounded on all sides by land. By contrast, this vessel rested on an odoriferous bed of muddy water, watery mud and debris. Muck. As rhymes with yuck.

"Is this another one of Arques' old ferryboats?" I asked Hank.

"You got it."

"This isn't where your president lives, is it?" The tone of my voice pleaded that the answer be no.

"Sure is. The *San Rafael*. That's where we're headed."

"Achille lives in *that?*"

"Yup."

"But it completely slopes to one side."

"It's not so bad once you get inside. It kind of tilts, but you get used to it."

"Really? But why does it look so strange? Why does it have that . . . tongue sticking out?"

"It was an auto ferry. The deck was where they parked the cars."

A long gangway, lacking any pretense of railings, led from the side of the dirt road to the protruding tongue. Below, primordial brown ooze lay in wait for the unwary pedestrian.

Pointing to the gangway, I asked warily, "Is this how we get aboard?"

"Sure is."

Two in front, two behind, me in the middle. My welcoming party wasn't taking any chances.

When we reached the protruding tongue, the gangway didn't end. Instead, it ran on top of the open deck all the way to the void space in back. A quick look down explained why. The deck had rotted to the point anyone walking on it would fall through.

The gangway ended inside the void space at a rickety, steep wood staircase. The staircase, like the rest of the boat, tilted to the left. The void space was dark and murky, the top of the staircase obscure. The air reeked — surprise, surprise — of rotting wood.

We headed up the steep, dark, off-kilter staircase. I silently wondered if things were going to keep getting worse and worse. Fortunately, a primitive wood handrail offered help on the downward side.

At the top of the stairway, a slanted door opened, murky light seeped out, and we entered a large, open, loft-like space, definitely sloped, filled with people and smoke.

Smells saturated the warm, stagnant air. The sweet scent of pipe tobacco. The gritty tang of cigarette smoke. The moldy, sour odors of rotting wood. A whiff of coffee.

The room's arrangement suggested a small theater, with the oddity that the floor sloped up toward the stage, instead of down. Fifteen or twenty people — young, white, male and female — were settled in, some in regular chairs, some in beanbag chairs, others simply sitting on the floor. All faced right, toward the uphill side of the room.

That uphill side conjured the library of an English country house. Three majestic floor-to-ceiling bookcases housed hundreds of richly bound, scholarly-looking books. On panels between the bookcases hung paintings darkened by old age. A small marble statue of a classically dressed woman holding a jar over her shoulder rested on a shelf.

Against this backdrop, framed on one side by a table covered with books and on the other by an old-fashioned shaded floor lamp, sat an elderly man with surprisingly abundant snow-white hair, a pink face, and a prominent, hooked nose. He wore a ragged brown shawl and had a pipe in his mouth.

I didn't need to ask who he was.

We headed up the slope, people scooting aside to open a path. When we reached the crest, Hank took over. "Mr. Spenser, I'd like to introduce you to Achille Palaiologos, the president of Save Our Waterfront. Achille, this is Rick Spenser, the lawyer from Legal Aid."

Achille reached out a thin, bony hand. "Good afternoon, Mr. Spenser. Or may I call you Rick?"

"Certainly."

"Rick, I hope you'll forgive me for not getting up, but my strength is not what it used to be."

"Please don't get up."

"But you be seated. Please, someone, find Rick a chair."

A rickety chair appeared, and I sat. Hank, Becky and Montse sat on the floor. Kevin remained standing, leaning against one of Achille's bookcases.

"Well then, good afternoon, Rick, and welcome to my home," Achille said. " I find it a lovely place to live. I hope you like it too."

To tell the truth, I didn't find his malodorous, off-plumb space lovely, but neither did I want to insult the tribal chief. "It's very interesting and unusual."

"And where are you from, Rick?"

Odd question. Most clients seeking help from Legal Aid don't ask where their prospective attorney is from. But no reason not to answer.

"Pasadena."

Achille chuckled. "I imagine you find Waldo Point somewhat different from Pasadena."

My turn to laugh. "Yes, definitely."

"Rick, I hope you can help us here at Waldo Point. For we face an onslaught of rampant capitalism that threatens our very existence.

"We have here what I dare say is one of the most idealistic and altruistic communities in the world today, a community that embodies the values of sharing, of giving, of caring for one another. This community has forged new paths in terms of respect for the environment, cultivation of self-sufficiency, and the practice of sustainable ways of life. This community welcomes anyone who wants to join and contribute. We do not turn away people. We do not discriminate. We do not say, 'You have a drinking problem and therefore we do not want you here.' Instead we say ..."

While Achille orated away, I noticed that seated on the floor next to his chair, underneath the floor lamp, was a sexy young woman with flowing red hair, clad in denim cut-offs and a yellow top that left her midriff bare. She held Achille's leg in her arms and was looking up at him in rapt admiration.

Achille was eighty-four. This woman looked to be in her mid-twenties, at most. One-third of eighty-four is twenty-eight. This woman wasn't even one-third Achille's age.

"... and for what reason?" the Byzantine Satyr was saying as I returned my attention to his words. "Greed. Pure capitalist greed. We have a group of rich investors, most of whom have probably never seen this historic place, never experienced the wonder of living on the water, never known the generous spirit of a community like ours. And these rich investors think that simply by reason of their money, their ill-gotten money, and because of the politicians they've managed to buy off, they think they can destroy this unique community, destroy it completely, take over the waters that by all right and law belong to the public, and make vast sums of money for themselves while turning Waldo Point into a collection of floating suburban homes filled with rich people like themselves.

"Nor is even that the full extent of their viciousness. They intend to change the name of this magical place from Waldo Point, the name by which it has been known since time immemorial, to Strawberry Point Harbor, after that little spit of land way up by Tiburon. In this way, they plan to eradicate not only us, but also our history. Mark my words, these rapacious capitalists will not rest until every last vestige of our community has been exterminated from the face of the earth.

"Rick, I hope, I desperately hope, you can help us avoid this tragic fate."

After this florid and lengthy start, I needed to take a businesslike tone. I explained that I was only one of three attorneys at Marin Legal Aid, that I by myself didn't have the authority to take on any case or commit Legal Aid to any sort of representation, and that all requests for the agency's assistance were funneled through a weekly meeting where all three attorneys took part.

I said I would bring up the Waldo Point situation at next week's attorneys' meeting and, based mainly on the reported fact that up to 160 low-income people were facing eviction, would ask for approval to explore the possibility — just the possibility — of representing SOW in a large-scale lawsuit again the county and the San Francisco developer. It was far too early, I emphasized, to expect Legal Aid to commit to bringing such a lawsuit. The most to be hoped for at the meeting next week was a go-ahead for further investigation. But I did think I could get my two colleagues to go along with that.

Silence followed my emotion-dampening presentation. Finally Achille spoke up.

"Rick, I'm sure you have rules you're supposed to follow and forms you're supposed to fill out. And that's all well and good. But it's important not to lose sight of what's at stake here."

Achille spread his arms, pipe in one hand. The puff of white hair surrounding his pink face looked like a fuzzy halo.

"What's at stake here is not just the survival of this community. We're unimportant. We're just a few souls who, probably foolishly, have tried to swim against the rising tide of capitalist destruction.

"What's really at stake here is the survival of the entire world. And I mean that in all seriousness. For if communities like ours cannot survive, if communities based on love and sharing and cooperation and charity toward others cannot survive in this desperate world, then truly there is no hope. Without communities like us, there is nothing to oppose the relentless force of capitalism as it turns the work place into a savage jungle, loots and destroys the environment, banishes creativity, and destroys the soul.

"I see only two alternatives. Either capitalist oppression totally obliterates communities like ours, and as a result completes its enslavement of the world. Or — and this is what I fervently *pray* will happen — communities like ours serve as a saving remnant, there to lead the world back to the values of the human spirit, and away from basing everything on money and greed."

Achille's youthful female companion grabbed his leg even tighter and gazed up at his face in wonderment.

"Right on!" shouted a voice behind me. I turned around. A husky young man with a red beard and red dreadlocks had stood up. He wore a tie-dye T-shirt so long it seemed more like a dress.

"Achille's got the skinny," the gentleman in tie-dye continued. "We gotta stand up to this shit. I mean, there's something fuckin' crazy goin' on here.

"I don't understand" — here he paused for dramatic effect, his eyes raised to the ceiling, his red dreadlocks hanging down his back, his arms spread and his palms up, as if in supplication — "how some bunch of rich bastards can say we don't have no right to live on the ocean. I don't understand how some bunch of rich bastards can say they *own* the ocean.

"I mean, this here, where we live, this is Richardson Bay, right? And Richardson Bay is connected to San Francisco Bay, right? And San Francisco Bay is connected to the Pacific Ocean, right? Well hell, the Pacific Ocean is connected to every other ocean in the whole damn world. The Indian, the Atlantic, all of 'em. Which means, it's all just *one big ocean.* Wherever you got one ocean, you got 'em all. And that's what we got here. We got the whole damn ocean right here at Waldo Point. Ain't that amazing? So if these assholes are saying they own Waldo Point, they're saying they own *the whole damn ocean.*"

As Mr. Tie-dye spoke on, I surveyed the crowd. Given the tight seating, fifty-fifty gender split, and perfectly timed youth of most of the women, I had rarely in my life seen such a dense concentration of female pulchritude. Beautiful hair, beautiful eyes, beautiful faces, beautiful shoulders, beautiful breasts — all abounded like spring wildflowers in a meadow. There were so many luscious young women, in fact, it was hard to focus on any one. Or on Mr. Tie-dye's meandering rant, for that matter.

"Man, Waldo Point is great," he was saying. "We got everything you need. We got drugs, we got girls, we got rock 'n' roll. Shit, what more do you need?"

I had to laugh along with all the others.

"Here at Waldo Point, you can do whatever you want to do, be whoever you want to be. And you know what we got that's the most important thing of all? The most important thing of all, which we got, is . . . *freedom!*"

A cheer rose from the crowd as Mr. Tie-dye sat down. At this point, my head full of too much talk and my lungs full of too much bad air, I said I needed to get back to my office. Achille and I bid each other farewell, he emphasizing he hoped to see me again. Becky, Kevin, Hank and Montse led me back out — down the slope and past the crowd to the door, down the steep, dark staircase, across the plank path laid atop the *San Rafael*'s rotting deck, and across the long gangway without railings.

Back on dry land, I asked, "Who was the guy in the tie-dye T-shirt?"

"Oh," Kevin said, "He's called Hashbury. That's because he came here from the Haight-Ashbury."

"And because he loves hash," Becky added in her low, sultry voice.

We took the dirt road back to where my car was parked. Montse, voluptuous Montse with her tinkling necklaces and bracelets, started walking beside me. "As you can see," she said, "we have a wide variety of people and viewpoints within our community. But that's what makes Waldo Point so special. We're different people, we have different philosophies, we want different things. But we all get along and help and support each other. We can be close to each other — physically, very close, as you've seen — but at the same time tolerate a wide range of differences. We can be friends with each other without having to control each other. That's so important, and so rare.

"And you know what makes it all work? It's love. That's the magic. What holds this community together is love."

Were the Beatles right? Was it true that all you needed was love?

Love seemed an all-conquering force that sunny, tranquil October day, with the members of the Waldo Point houseboat community enjoying themselves on their boats, working on community projects, or camped at the feet of their guru, Achille. But would love be enough in troubled times, which unfortunately seemed to lie ahead?

5
TIFFANY

Tiffany arrived at my San Rafael apartment around seven that evening.

That was our arrangement at the time. Tiffany spent Friday and Saturday nights at my place in Marin, and we enjoyed the weekend together. Sunday evenings she went back to her apartment in the Richmond District of San Francisco, an apartment she shared with two other women, both, like herself, Chinese-American. During the week Tiffany worked at an art gallery in downtown San Francisco.

"So, how did your afternoon with the houseboat people go?" she asked while we were still in our first embrace.

I sighed and shook my head. "Hard to sum up in just a few words. At this point I'm not sure what I think."

Still holding me, she tilted her head back and said with a sly smile, "Were there a lot of beautiful white babes there?"

How did she know? Why was this the first thing she asked?

"Tiffany," I said in the most sincere tone I could muster, "I was there on business. I didn't have time to notice the physical attributes of the women I met."

What a lie.

"Oh, I bet there were lots of beautiful white girls there with big beautiful white boobs." She pressed herself against me.

This was a subject on which Tiffany wasted too much thought. She was sensitive that she, like most Asian women, didn't have the large breasts she thought all

American men wanted. Many times I had assured her I loved her breasts just as they were, but she never quite seemed to believe me.

"Tiffany, I didn't ask the female members of Save Our Waterfront to take their clothes off."

"But I bet you wished you could!" She pressed her body into mine, put her hands into the back pockets of my jeans, and pulled my pelvis toward her body. This was a signature move of hers that always set my hormones raging.

Consider my predicament. I had spent the afternoon surrounded by an unprecedented concentration of foxy young women, not just the entrancing Becky, but also Montse and a score of others in Achille's audience chamber. Now I was being pressed like laminate into the sexiest body part of a woman I found irresistibly attractive. I was — can you blame me? — very, very horny.

"Tiff, let's head into the bedroom."

"Now? I haven't even unpacked."

"You can unpack later. I'm so happy to see you."

"Even after all those gorgeous white women with their big white boobs that you met this afternoon?"

"I don't remember anything about it. I'm just so happy to see you."

"Well, all right."

Our lovemaking was passionate, but perhaps too speedy.

Lying in bed afterward, in that languid period after sex when time seems to stand still, into my mind floated the image of Becky. Her long curly blond hair. Her supple, slender body. Her suntanned arms and legs. Her electric fuchsia dress.

What the hell? Why, just after I'd made love to someone I considered the most sublime woman in the world, was I thinking about *another* woman?

Maybe I needed to be honest with myself. Even though I'd met her only two times, Becky had made a strong impression on me.

Odd I should be attracted to both Becky and Tiffany. Physically, they were opposites. Did I not have a "type"?

Actually, Becky and Tiffany weren't *total* opposites. In body type they were similar: Becky was slender for a white woman, and her breasts weren't much larger than Tiffany's. But in terms of surfaces — hair, eyes, skin — they were opposites.

Becky had golden hair, skin the color of honey, forest-green eyes. Tiffany had . . . It was conventional to say Chinese women had olive skin. But Tiffany didn't look like an olive to me. Not at all. More like . . . Perhaps a piece of silk. Meaning not a particular color, but a texture. Smooth, lustrous —

"I'm hungry." Tiffany's voice derailed my train of thought.

We decided to splurge and were able to snag a reservation at the Fish Peddler in San Rafael harbor.

The hostess seated us at a table next to the window wall overlooking the yacht harbor. The harbor's lights twinkled and reflected onto the water, and the masts of the sailboats swayed in the wind.

Over dinner I gave Tiffany a detailed account of my afternoon at Waldo Point, leaving out only my impressions of the women. When I was done, she asked, "The people there, were they all, like, one hundred percent white?"

I tried to recall. Montse was probably Hispanic. Other than that . . .

"Basically, yes."

Tiffany pursed her lips, as if to say, "Exactly what I expected."

After dinner we finished our wine gazing out at the yacht harbor. Achille and Hashbury would hate this place, I thought. The lights hung in a straight line, the pretty boats neatly lined up alongside straight docks. It reeked of rich people, luxury, suburbia. Achille would absolutely hate it.

But for Tiffany and me, seeking and deserving a romantic evening to top off the workweek, it was perfect. Tiffany glowed in the dim lighting of the restaurant and the reflected light of the yacht harbor. She did indeed look silken.

We sat for a while in silence. Finally Tiffany said, "You know what your trip to the *San Rafael* and that guy Achille reminds me of?"

"No. What?"

"Conrad. *Heart of Darkness.*"

I had to think for a moment. "Oh, you mean Kurtz? You're equating Achille and Kurtz?"

"Precisely."

I took another sip of my chardonnay. "Interesting."

Again a romantic silence came over us. Again it was Tiffany who broke the silence.

"I seem to remember that in *Heart of Darkness* Kurtz and his followers held, and I think I'm quoting this accurately, 'midnight dances with unspeakable rites.' Do you think your houseboat people hold midnight dances with unspeakable rites?"

"I wouldn't be at all surprised."

We both laughed and took another sip of our wine.

But on the way home, a disturbing thought crept into my mind. In *Heart of Darkness,* wasn't Kurtz's compound surrounded by a palisade of severed heads on stakes?

6
ATTORNEYS' MEETING

I was the last to arrive at our attorneys' meeting the next week. Sam, my boss, and Judith, the other staff attorney, were already seated. Tall, thin Sam, with his usual frazzled look. Tiny, pale, redheaded Judith, with her usual frown.

The room, our combination library, conference room and lunchroom, bore aromas of pickles and onions, along with the mustiness of used law books and the bite of cigarette smoke. I pushed aside a tall stack of opened law books to make room for myself at the rickety table that filled the room's center. The table served as burial ground for numerous half-completed research projects, including several of my own. Two paralegals were at work, or at least pretending to be at work, at the other end of the table.

At our weekly attorneys' meeting, the three of us went over all the cases that had come in during the prior week and decided how we would handle, or not handle, each of them. To some people we simply gave advice. Some people we equipped with a *pro per* answer they could file on their own. To some people we simply said, "Sorry, but we can't help you." And in a relatively small percentage of cases, we agreed to represent the client in court.

At today's meeting, I wasn't hoping for approval of a large-scale lawsuit on behalf of Save Our Waterfront. It was far too premature for that; after all, I hadn't done any legal research. But I was hoping to get the go-ahead for continuing to work with the houseboat community, exploring the possibility of such a suit.

Over the weekend, I'd become more and more convinced theirs was a cause Legal Aid should embrace. I kept coming back to one overriding fact. The new owner of Waldo Point was planning to evict 160 persons. All of us working at Marin Legal Aid were very much aware there were embarrassingly few poor people in Marin County. Moreover, the number of poor Marin residents seemed to be shrinking precipitously as the county's 1970s real estate boom shifted into overdrive. A loss of 160 persons — and it was a reasonable assumption most residents of Waldo Point were low-income — would be major.

I also had personal reasons for wanting to continue with the houseboaters. The thought of helming a major lawsuit on behalf of the legendary Waldo Point houseboat community was tantalizing. I'd only been in practice three years, and while I'd worked in a junior capacity on several major cases, here, for the first time, I would be lead attorney. I'd be representing an exotic and probably interesting group of clients. And I couldn't help thinking that if Legal Aid said "no" to the houseboaters, I'll probably never see Becky again.

I realized it wasn't going to be easy to convince my two colleagues. Judith would almost certainly be opposed. She prided herself on being the champion of the downtrodden, but her definition of "the downtrodden" was strict. By and large, white people, except for single mothers and the extremely old, didn't qualify.

As for Sam, his one previous experience with the Waldo Point community — representing Sandra-something-or-other, the druggie "hitchhiker" — was negative. Plus, with him, there was always the memory of the Marin Highlands case, even though it was now two years in the past.

In the Marin Highlands case, Legal Aid brought a suit uncomfortably similar to what the houseboaters were asking for now — Legal Aid, representing a group of low-income persons, suing the County of Marin and a big-bucks private developer over an issue of development. No sooner had the Marin Highlands case been filed than everything went wrong. The Marin County Board of Supervisors, who provided part of our funding, erupted in rage. Some of the plaintiffs changed their minds and dropped out of the suit. The case began consuming so much of the office's time we couldn't take on any new cases. People began to complain, our Legal Aid board became involved, and Sam almost lost his job. He didn't want to repeat that experience.

Sam looked up from his paperwork. "We may as well start with the most controversial," he said, looking at me. "Tell us about your adventures with the Waldo Point people."

I went over, as concisely as I could, everything I'd learned about the houseboat community. I tried to present the negative as well as the positive, but steered my presentation toward getting approval to continue working with the houseboaters. I admitted I hadn't done any legal research so far, and confirmed we wouldn't file suit against two formidable opponents like the County of Marin and a deep-pocketed San Francisco development group unless there were good legal grounds for doing so.

"Do you have any idea what those grounds might be?" Sam asked. "It isn't obvious to me."

"I know there is, or at least was, such a thing under California law as a right of navigation, and this right of navigation includes a right of anchorage. But I don't know how this applies to houseboats. Also, there was a permit issued a few years ago, and where there's a permit there's generally an Environmental Impact Report, and where there's an EIR there's generally some legal issue or another. But as of the moment, this is just speculation on my part."

Sam nodded. "One other question before I turn it over to Judith. You say these people are being evicted. But I didn't hear you talk about any unlawful detainers. Nobody at Waldo Point has been served with a UD yet, is that correct?"

Unlawful detainer — UD — was the type of lawsuit that, under California law, landlords used to evict tenants.

"Correct. The whole idea behind this big lawsuit against the county and the developer is to strike first and that way be on the offensive. If we just wait around for the developer to begin serving unlawful detainers, we'll always be on the defensive. Furthermore, everybody will be busy defending his or her own individual UD, and the group, SOW, will fall apart."

Sam twirled his pen between his index and middle fingers, his usual nervous habit. Finally he turned to Judith and asked, "What do you think?"

Judith was already glaring at me. "You said three people from this so-called community showed up at our offices last week. Is that right?"

"Yes."

"Did they fill out applications?"

"Yes."

"Could I see them?"

Fortunately, I'd remember to bring Becky, Kevin and Hank's application forms. I handed them to Judith.

She studied them for a full minute, while the rest of us watched in silence. Then, looking up, she asked, "Were all three of these people white?"

"Yes."

"Did they all look healthy? Did any of them seem disabled?"

48

"Yes, they all looked healthy." I thought of Becky and her sun-tanned shoulders and arms. "And none of them seemed to have any obvious disabilities."

"Did you see any reason why, if they maybe cleaned themselves up and cut their hair, they couldn't go out and get a job that would put them well above the poverty level?"

For such a tiny woman, she packed a mean punch.

It took me a while to settle on an answer. Finally I said, "Isn't it also true, Judith, that if *you* went out and really applied yourself, you could get yourself a higher-paying position than your current job at Marin Legal Aid?"

She glared at me, waiting for Sam to chastise me. He didn't. The two paralegals at the other end of the table watched intently. They always seemed to love it when the knives came out.

Judith again looked slowly through the three application forms. She picked out one and said, "This guy is white, twenty-eight years old, and he says he's unemployed and has zero income. What is he, an unemployed philosopher? I'll bet he's a drug dealer."

The same thought about Kevin had occurred to me earlier. But by now, that thought had been superseded by my ardent desire to continue working with the houseboaters. My first chance to be lead attorney on a major case. The cool factor in representing the legendary Waldo Point houseboat community. Becky. It was all too exciting, too promising, just to be tossed aside after a brief discussion in a single afternoon.

"You have no basis for saying that."

"Whether or not this guy is a drug dealer, we do have a rule that we're not supposed to represent the voluntary poor. And from everything I've heard, those people who live in houseboats down there at Waldo Point are prototypical examples of the voluntary poor. Mr. Kevin Cassidy included."

Sam was smiling, apparently enjoying Judith's and my sparring. I had a sense he was on my side. Beneath his bureaucratic exterior, he was actually fairly adventurous.

"Judith, look at it this way," I said. "There aren't that many poor people in Marin County, and they're mainly concentrated in four small enclaves — Marin City, the Canal District, San Quentin Prison and the houseboat area. For better or for worse, we already have a policy we don't take any cases from San Quentin. Now you're saying we shouldn't take any cases from the houseboat area? So are you saying we should limit ourselves to only two of the four areas where poor people live in Marin County?"

"What I'm saying is that even today we have truly poor people — people of color, single mothers on welfare, seniors — coming into this office, and we don't have the resources to take care of them all. Add some massive new lawsuit on behalf of a bunch of hippies, and we may as well put up a sign over the door saying, 'No truly poor people allowed.'"

There you had it. The houseboaters were undeserving of legal representation because they were hippies. Judith reminded me of Mayor Daley at the 1968 Democratic Convention. I looked to Sam for some help.

"Judith brings up a good point," Sam said, and my heart sank. "If we're going to jump into this thing, we need to know who these people are. I mean, are they all low-income? We're assuming they are, but other than the fact that three people came in last week and apparently qualified, or at least two of them did, we don't have any proof.

"What I can envision is we get into this thing, it blows up, our board gets all involved, and at some point they ask the question, 'Where's your documentation these people are low-income?' What do we say at that point? Do we hand them these three applications and say that's it?"

By now my heart had recovered. Sam's concern was perfectly valid, and he didn't seem hung up on the voluntary-poor issue. His saying Judith had a good point was just his way of letting her save face.

"You're right," I said. "I'll have to think of a way to address that issue."

Sam sat silently, looking down, twirling his pen between his index and middle fingers. Tiny Judith had sunk so low in her chair that all I could see were her red hair, scowling freckled forehead, and horn-rimmed glasses. I was worried Sam was going to return to the voluntary-poor issue.

"I remember after the Marin Highlands case," he finally said, causing me to tense, "I swore to myself we'd never again get into anything that big with defendants that well-funded unless we had somebody else working with us. We can't be the only attorneys for the plaintiffs; there have to be others. Did the people you talked to give any indication they were seeking other sources of legal help?"

"No, but they didn't say they weren't." I was happy the voluntary-poor issue had apparently died for lack of a second, but Sam's new concern was worrisome.

"Okay, then you need to tell them they have to start looking. Tell them Legal Aid might be willing to man one oar, but they've got to come up with some other oarsmen. They should understand the maritime analogy."

"They have to come up with more than one other attorney?"

"Not necessarily. We don't need to decide that now. Let's see who they come up with."

"Okay. But getting back to the question of whether any unlawful detainers have been served at Waldo Point, if a UD comes in from there, we'll take it, assuming the defendant is eligible, right?"

"Right."

"You want to funnel any houseboat UD that comes in to me?"

"I wasn't planning on funneling them to Judith." We both smiled at her. She didn't reciprocate.

"Okay," Sam said. "You'll look into this thing and report back. I'm curious what you'll find."

Later that day I phoned Kevin to talk to him about the two issues Sam raised. When I explained to Kevin that Legal Aid needed proof that the members of SOW, or at least a majority, were low-income, he had an immediate answer.

"That problem's being solved as we speak. We're doing a survey of all our members, asking them how much they make, how much they could afford to pay for a berth, and a bunch of other questions. We can get all that information to you in a couple of weeks."

When I raised the issue of the need for another attorney to share the load, Kevin again didn't miss a beat. "Glad you brought that up. It so happens we're talking to a professor at Golden Gate University who's a specialist in environmental law. He thinks we may have a case that the county needs to do an SEIR, Supplemental Environmental Impact Report, for the Waldo Point project. He's looking through a ton of documents now, and if he continues to think we have a good case, he's willing to work for us pro bono."

"Okay. That sounds promising. But let me make it clear that Legal Aid needs more than just a professor who's looking things over. We need someone who will commit to handling a substantial portion of the case."

"Understood."

Although I'd been stern to Kevin at the end, I was actually delighted to learn the houseboaters were showing more resourcefulness than I'd expected. I was also relieved our attorneys' meeting had gone so well.

More and more, it was looking as if the proposed big Waldo Point lawsuit might become a reality. For the first time in my fledgling legal career, I would be lead attorney, or at least co-lead attorney, on a major case. And I would be representing the infamous, exotic Waldo Point houseboat community.

I was stoked, I was psyched.

But in truth, I knew little of what I was getting into.

7
INSIDE VIEW

As a Legal Aid attorney, I had few friends inside the Marin County Civic Center. Legal Aid and the power structure at the Civic Center were natural enemies.

But I had made one at least semi-friend in county counsel's office, a low-ranking deputy my age named Sheryl Harding. On Monday I called her and asked if she knew anything about the Waldo Point situation. She did indeed; in fact, she'd worked on the permit. Would she be willing to spare a few minutes of her time and clue me in on how the county viewed the state of affairs? Yes, I could drop by her office in the Civic Center the next day.

I thought my office was ugly. At least it had a window, albeit a window that overlooked a parking lot and another two-story stucco office building just like mine. Sheryl's office, no bigger than mine, had no window, only a glass clerestory between her office and an interior corridor. Sheryl was the type of lawyer who covered every available surface, including the floor, with piles of files and books.

"Have a seat," she said, moving a pile of books off the one guest chair in her office. "So the houseboaters managed to find their way to Legal Aid?"

Sheryl was blonde and light, reasonably attractive, but with a certain hardness — perhaps features too sharp or a jawbone too strong — that for me took away her sex appeal.

"Yes, not only did they find their way to Legal Aid, I managed to find my way to Waldo Point."

"Well, I'm glad it didn't burn up while you were there. What did you think of the smell?"

I paused. Sheryl seemed more hardline than I remembered. "Does seem like there are some code violations down there."

"Look, Rick. If Legal Aid wants to help the houseboat people, that's your decision. I can't stop you, nor would I want to. But there's one thing you've got to understand. The train's out of the station on this one, and there's no stopping it. Waldo Point is going to be cleaned up. The plan we've all worked on so hard is going to be implemented."

"What about the people there now?"

"I hate to be the bearer of bad news, but those people are all going to be gone in two years."

I slumped in my chair, not sure what to say.

Sheryl took my silence as opportunity to strike another blow. "Another thing you need to know is that Ken has said cleaning up Waldo Point is going to be his legacy. His legacy to the people of Marin County."

Ken was Ken Ricciarelli, Marin County Counsel, Sheryl's boss and the man widely regarded as the most powerful figure in county government. At all the Board of Supervisors meetings I'd attended, Ricciarelli, sitting at a large desk next to the board, had, as each item on the agenda came up, given the board instructions, packaged as "legal advice," on how to vote. The board had invariably followed Ricciarelli's instructions. Having Ken Ricciarelli as your sworn enemy was not something you wanted in Marin County.

"Why does Ken hate the houseboaters so much?"

"Isn't it obvious? The fire hazard. The health hazard. The liability facing the county. Maybe you don't do municipal law, but public entities can get the crap sued out of them if there's a big disaster and it can be proven they weren't enforcing their building or health codes."

Sheryl's windowless office, with its malignant piles of books and papers, pressed in on me like a vise. There was no point arguing with her; she'd obviously made up her mind about the houseboat people. But maybe I could salvage something out of this meeting by picking her brain on some legal issues.

"One thing you might be able to clarify for me. The houseboat people keep asking me how can anyone own the ocean. And I don't know the answer to that. How is it that this Strawberry Point Harbor Associates group can claim to own a part of Richardson Bay, which after all, is a part of the Pacific Ocean?"

"Sure, I can answer that. In the 1870s the State of California set up something called the Board of Tideland Commissioners. The purpose of this agency was to subdivide the tidelands of San Francisco Bay so they could be sold to private investors and developed.

"The main place the Board of Tideland Commissioners did this was what's now downtown San Francisco. Remember that originally the waters of San Francisco Bay came all the way up to Montgomery Street, where the Transamerica Pyramid is now. Everything east of that, clear to the current waterfront, was tideland. The Board of Tideland Commissioners sold off this entire area to private developers, who proceeded to fill and develop it.

"The same thing happened in Richardson Bay, but with one big difference. The Board of Tideland Commissioners subdivided the tidelands and sold parcels to private parties. But here, for whatever reason or reasons, the private owners *didn't* fill or develop their tidelands. Instead, they just let them lie fallow, Donlon Arques being a prime example of this. But the sales were still valid, so whatever it may look like to the naked eye, the tidelands of Richardson Bay, including the Arques property, are private property. Title to the Arques property is just as secure as title to all the big office buildings and hotels in downtown San Francisco. Legally, they're identical."

"Okay," I said, taking notes. "Another thing the houseboaters talk about is a right of navigation, which they say includes a right of anchorage. Are you familiar with a right of navigation or right of anchorage?"

"I'm generally aware that a right of navigation exists. I've never heard of a right of anchorage, but I can see how it might follow from a right of navigation. In any event, I'm not aware of any California case in which the right of navigation has been applied to houseboats. Are you aware of any such case?"

"To be honest, I haven't done any library research yet. All I've done is talked to some of the people and visited."

"Well, I'll be very surprised if you find anything. Hard to see why the right of navigation should apply to a houseboat, when by definition a houseboat is a vessel that can't move under its own power."

I'd had enough of Sheryl's bad news by this point. I said I needed to get back to my office, thanked her for her help, and got up to leave.

She escorted me to the door. "It's great you're working with the houseboaters. Lord knows they need help. But take some advice from a friend. Don't get emotionally involved. Keep your distance. Their cause is a real loser."

8
UNLAWFUL DETAINER

I returned from a welfare hearing at the Civic Center to find the entire office abuzz. While I was gone, an unlawful detainer — eviction lawsuit — from Waldo Point had walked in the door. The client had filled out an application form and been deemed eligible. We were taking the case, and I was in charge.

Damn, I thought, there goes our strategy. The houseboaters and I had planned on striking first, filing suit against the country and Strawberry Point Harbor Associates before they filed any eviction actions. That way, hopefully, we could avoid getting bogged down in a myriad of individual eviction cases and watching the developer's bigger bucks overwhelm our limited means. Now, before we were even half-organized, the parade of unlawful detainers had already begun.

Unfortunately, the UD client and the people he came with — probably the usual Houseboat Three, I surmised — were already gone, not wanting to wait around for my time-uncertain return. But they left behind not just a stack of papers, but also a note inviting me to dinner that evening on the client's houseboat.

My eyebrows went up. Not the usual start to a Legal Aid attorney-client relationship. But with the houseboaters, nothing was by the rulebook.

I grabbed the papers and hurried to my office. I first looked at the application form. The client's name was Justin Lambert, and his address was the Owl, Gate 5, Waldo Point.

The Owl! The strange-looking boat I had glimpsed on my tour last week, supposedly the masterpiece of some well known — at least on the waterfront — boat sculptor. Reading on, Justin Lambert was twenty-nine and a sculptor. Apparently not a very successful sculptor, for his income was only four hundred a month.

With Tiffany in San Francisco, I had no dinner plans that weekday night. I was eager to meet my new client, and frankly curious about the Owl. I immediately called the number on the invitation to confirm. A woman answered, obviously not the client, and said all would be ready.

That afternoon I managed to squeeze in some quick-and-dirty research on the right of navigation. The good news was that the 1873 California Supreme Court case that Hank brought to my attention had never been reversed. Ever since 1873, the language Hank had underlined — confirming a right of navigation, including a right of anchorage — was repeated verbatim every five or ten years by some appellate court or another. The bad news was that there was no case applying the right of anchorage to a houseboat situation, or anything even remotely resembling a houseboat situation.

I arrived at the Waldo Point dirt parking lot exactly on time. I expected to see the usual trio, but only Kevin greeted me. I asked where the other two were.

"There are some logistical issues getting to the Owl. You'll see in a minute."

I wondered what "logistical issues" meant. Flimsier floating docks? Even more perilous gangways? But I decided best not to ask. Fortunately, dinner was set early, so it was still light.

As we walked down the dirt road toward Gate 5, Kevin had news for me. SOW's survey of Waldo Point residents was almost done. Not only that, in the course of conducting the survey they'd discovered there was a lawyer living in their midst, and this lawyer was willing, indeed eager, to participate in the proposed big lawsuit against the county and the developer.

I wondered what type of lawyer would choose to live at Waldo Point, but kept this thought to myself.

Kevin had more good news. The environmental law professor at Golden Gate University had committed to putting together the California Environmental Quality Act section of the lawsuit. The conditions that Sam, my directing attorney, had set for Legal Aid's jumping in were rapidly being met.

Before we reached the *San Rafael*, Achille's home, we turned left onto a rickety walkway that took us over a long stretch of smelly muck. The walkway ended where the muck turned into deep water. A small dock stuck out, and beside the dock floated a rowboat. Standing on the dock was a tall, slender man with long, black hair and a short beard. He wore a loose-fitting shirt and baggy pants, both of white linen, sandals, and a saffron-colored flower lei around his neck.

"Is that Justin Lambert?" I asked Kevin.

"That is he."

Justin Lambert invited Kevin and me to sit on one bench of the rowboat; he took the other bench and rowed. I now understood what Kevin had meant by "logistical issues." It would have been hard to fit five into this rowboat.

Justin threaded the rowboat through a group of smaller houseboats until finally the Owl soared up ahead of us. It was indeed spectacular, at least thirty feet tall, made entirely of wood planks, most of them bent, a symphony of curves and circles. The main part of the vessel consisted of a teepee-shaped structure punctuated by three round vertically aligned windows. Behind the teepee loomed an upward-facing wooden arc, the two pointed ends of the arc conjuring an owl's two ears. At the bottom of the teepee a circular opening suggested an owl's mouth and offered a way in.

"It's quite something. Who did you say built it?"

"Chris Roberts," Kevin answered, as Justin continued to row. "He also designed another very cool boat called the Madonna. Unfortunately, it burned about four years ago."

"Was anyone killed?"

"No, thank God."

The news of a major fire at Waldo Point didn't bode well for a lawsuit aimed at stopping, or at least slowing down, redevelopment. I thought of what Sheryl Harding said when I'd told her I'd visited Waldo Point. "Glad it didn't burn up while you were there."

In front of the Owl a small dock stuck out, and Justin eased the rowboat beside it. Strangely, despite my excitement over at last stepping onto the legendary Owl, I had a growing sense of unease. I couldn't quite put my finger on it, but something was wrong. Out of tact, I said nothing.

A gangway, fortunately with railings on both sides, led to the circular opening, the mouth. We stepped through. I did a double take.

I was on a balcony. And the balcony looked down on water. The same muddy brown water we'd just been traversing by rowboat.

"Um, could somebody explain to me . . ."

For a second, Kevin looked puzzled. Then he laughed and said, "Oh. Nobody told you the Owl was sunk? I'm sorry. I just thought you knew. Anyway, the Owl, the poor Owl, is sunk. It's been that way for a couple of years. You're looking at what used to be the main floor, but now it's covered in about six feet of water."

Great. As if it weren't enough of an uphill struggle to argue that the right of navigation applied to a floating houseboat, now I was supposed to argue that the right of navigation applied to a sunken houseboat.

Perhaps it was time to say goodbye to the right-of-navigation argument.

I stood silent for a moment, mourning the demise of the one legal argument I'd brought with me. But eventually my attention shifted to the strange interior space that surrounded me.

Strong incense filled the air, blessedly masking the rank odor of the water that now occupied the Owl's lower story. Sitar music emanated from an unknown source.

Looking up, I realized I was inside the teepee-like structure I'd seen from the outside. The walls were constructed entirely of wood planks — the same wood planks, in fact, I'd seen from the outside; the Owl was only one wood plank thick. The funnel-shaped top of the teepee now seemed immeasurably far away, and what had looked like windows from the outside were now skylights.

The enormous number of wood planks making up the towering, thirty-foot-high structure defied comprehension. Not only that, being surrounded 360 degrees by wood planks arranged in a circle felt . . . well, creepy. It was like being shut inside a gigantic wine barrel.

Returning my gaze to level, I saw that the balcony, which was now the Owl's only habitable story, had been transformed into something approaching a functioning household. I was standing in an area with a table, a few pillows and a small bookcase — no chairs. To my left, a captivating dark-skinned young woman in a purple sari was preparing food in a small, makeshift kitchen. Across the way could be seen the outlines of a bed. And to my right, set by itself, stood an altar bearing a dancing Shiva surrounded by offerings of flowers and fruits.

Still, the void at the center, the water where the first floor should have been, was hard to ignore. True, a sturdy railing surrounded the drop-off, and true, when sitting on the floor you couldn't actually see the water. But you knew it was there. You knew you were sunk.

Justin's sari-clad girlfriend, introduced as Asha, began serving food. And delicious food it was, Indian vegetarian — lentils, eggplant, okra, cauliflower — all cooked in rich, spicy sauces.

About halfway through the meal I realized that so far I'd totally failed to act like a lawyer handling an unlawful detainer, which was the purpose of my visit. Time to get to work.

"What's your rent here, Justin? Or do you call it berthage?"

"I don't pay rent."

"You don't pay rent? None at all?"

"Nope."

"Have you ever paid any rent?"

"Never."

"How have you been getting away with that?"

"Nobody's ever asked me to."

"Really?"

"Really."

I paused to gather my thoughts. Despite having handled scores of unlawful detainers, I'd never received answers like this before.

"Okay, let's go back to the beginning. When did you move here?"

"I moved to Waldo Point in 1969. But I didn't live on the Owl then. I lived on a boat up in Gate 6. I bought the Owl in February of 1973."

"Okay, did you at around that time . . . Let me start over. Do you know Donlon Arques?"

"I know who he is. I wouldn't consider us personal friends."

"Did you, at around the time you bought the Owl, have any conversations with Donlon Arques about that fact?"

"Yes, I did."

"And do you remember what was said?"

"I told him I'd bought the Owl from Chris Roberts."

"And what did Arques say?"

"He said, 'Take good care of her. She's a beauty.'"

"Was that all?"

"That was all."

"Have you had any conversations with Donlon Arques since then?"

"When we see each other we say hello."

"Nothing more than that?"

"We might say, 'Looks like it's going to rain,' or something like that."

"But nothing about your occupying the Owl, or about paying rent?"

"No."

Again I paused. An idea was beginning to take shape in my mind, but it wasn't fully formed. I needed more facts.

"Did Arques have any sort of assistant, like a property manager or a harbormaster?" I looked at both Justin and Kevin.

"He had a harbormaster," Kevin answered. "Guy named D. B. Luther."

"Is this D. B. Luther still around?"

"He is, and I should warn you. He now works for Strawberry Point Harbor Associates. He went over to the dark side."

I turned back to Justin. "Did you have any conversations with D. B. Luther?"

"No. I've never talked to him. I don't think he likes me."

"Why do you say that?"

"Just the way he looks at me whenever he sees me."

"That might explain why you're the first to get an unlawful detainer."

"I thought of that myself."

I took out my yellow pad and started making notes. Then I asked Justin, "You've heard of Strawberry Point Harbor Associates, haven't you?"

"Of course."

"Have you ever had any conversations with anyone from Strawberry Point Harbor Associates?"

"No. I wouldn't recognize them if I saw them."

By now, the idea in my head had evolved into a clear legal strategy.

Unlawful detainer was a very specialized type of lawsuit under California law. Basically, it was designed to enable landlords to evict tenants speedily. From a landlord's standpoint, the advantages of unlawful detainer were twofold. First, the defendant's answer had to be filed within five days after service, as opposed to thirty days in a regular lawsuit. Second, unlawful detainers were given first priority in court scheduling, which meant they normally came to trial within a week or so after the filing of the answer, whereas a regular lawsuit might wait two to three years before getting a trial date.

But there were various prerequisites to filing an unlawful detainer, and one of them — an obvious, unquestioned prerequisite — was the existence of a landlord-tenant relationship. From everything Justin was saying, it didn't appear a landlord-tenant relationship had ever been established between Arques and him. Or between Strawberry Point Harbor Associates and him.

The idea seemed too good to be true. I'd never heard of anyone winning an unlawful detainer based on lack of a landlord-tenant relationship. I needed to cross-examine Justin some more. There had to be a flaw.

I looked at him. With his long black hair, wispy beard, large eyes, loose-fitting white linen clothing and flower lei, he looked exactly like photos I'd seen of George Harrison in India.

Putting this distraction to the side, I reached into my briefcase, pulled out the complaint, and said to him, "Look. It says here in paragraph three, 'On or about November 1, 1972, plaintiff' — meaning Donlon Arques — 'and defendant' — that's you — 'entered into an agreement for the rental of a parcel of real property approximately forty feet by thirty feet located at Gate Five, Waldo Point, County of Marin.' Is that true?"

"Could you read it again?"

I read it again.

"No, that's absolutely not true. In fact, it's ridiculous. It says I did this in November of 1972. I didn't even buy the Owl until February of 1973."

"Can you prove that?"

He thought for a moment, then said, "I think so." He got up from the floor, and circled the balcony toward what appeared to be the bedroom. While he was gone, I had a chance to exchange small talk with his dark-haired, sari-clad, talented-cook girlfriend.

Justin came back with a sheet of paper. It was a bill of sale, signed by Chris Roberts. The Chris Roberts. At the top, in the same ink as his signature, was a skillful drawing of the Owl. As Tiffany would say, an original Chris Roberts pen-and-ink drawing. More to the point, there was a date on the bill of sale. February 15, 1973. Justin was telling the truth.

At that point I explained to Justin, Kevin and Asha my legal strategy — that we could possibly win the unlawful detainer based on lack of a landlord-tenant relationship. I also warned, which I had to, that winning the unlawful detainer would not mean Justin could stay in his current spot forever. Strawberry Point Harbor Associates could bring an action in ejectment, which required proof of only two things, first, that the defendant was on your property, and second, that you wanted him off. No need to prove any landlord-tenant relationship. However, an ejectment action had lowest priority for trial scheduling, so even if Strawberry Point Harbor Associates filed an ejectment action against Justin immediately, it wouldn't come to trial for two or three years.

This having been explained, I set to work on trial preparation. "Who's going to appear on behalf of Strawberry Point Harbor Associates?"

"What do you mean?" Kevin replied.

"Strawberry Point Harbor Associates is the plaintiff. That means they go first. They have to put somebody on the witness stand to testify to all the allegations in the complaint, including the allegation that a landlord-tenant relationship was established. My question is: who is that individual going to be?"

Both Kevin and Justin looked baffled.

"Is it going to be Donlon Arques?" I asked. "Would he be willing to be Strawberry Point Harbor Associates' star witness?"

Kevin shook his head. "I can't see that at all. He's not the type for courts or lawsuits. In fact, I've never seen him in anything but overalls and work boots. Plus, he has no love for Strawberry Point Harbor Associates. He didn't want to sell to them. He only did it because the county forced him to. You agree, Justin?"

Justin agreed.

"Okay, if not Arques, then who? You mentioned somebody, a J. D. — "

"D. B. Luther," said Kevin. He and Justin looked at each other unsurely. "I guess he's as likely as anyone."

"Tell me something about D. B. Luther. Is he honest?"

"He used to be, when he worked for Arques. But I don't know now that he works for Strawberry Point Harbor Associates."

"It would be nice if he were."

After dinner was finished and I'd asked all the questions I could think of, I began packing up to leave. But there was one other matter I needed to attend to.

I looked at Justin, attired as he was in his baggy white linen shirt and pants, flower lei, and sandals. "Um, Justin, for your trial, do you think you could dress a little more . . . middle American?"

He looked down, fingered his saffron-colored lei, then looked at me and said, smiling, "I'll try."

9
THE TRIAL OF THE OWL

Justin Lambert was true to his word. He showed up for his trial clad in a cotton dress shirt, jeans, shoes and no lei. He also brought with him his original bill of sale for the Owl from Chris Roberts, our ace in the hole if the witness who appeared on behalf of Strawberry Point Harbor Associates was willing to lie.

About twenty other Waldo Point residents came to the trial, including Becky, Kevin, Hank, Montse and Asha. No Achille or Hashbury though. I took the strong turnout as a good sign. Maybe there was truth to Montse's repeated claims the houseboat community was like a big family.

Shortly before trial was scheduled to begin, four men walked into the courtroom. "That's D. B. Luther," said Kevin. "The old guy following behind."

D. B. Luther, former right-hand man to Arques, now apparently front man for Strawberry Point Harbor Associates, was a thin, deeply-weathered, tired-looking man, with a few strands of grey hair and wire-rim spectacles. His sports coat, shirt and pants looked as if they'd been plucked from the Salvation Army bin.

I recognized another man in the group, an attorney I'd often seen around the Marin County courts. He generally represented local landlords and small businesses, and thus it was hard to believe he was chief attorney for Strawberry Point Harbor Associates, a big-time real estate development group out of San Francisco. He was probably brought in just to handle this eviction.

A look at the third member of the group confirmed that hypothesis. His grey pinstriped suit looked extravagantly expensive, as if it had come from Wilkes Bashford, and his face expressed hauteur bordering on disdain. "I'll bet that guy is Strawberry Point Harbor Associates' *chief* lawyer," I said to Kevin. He agreed.

The fourth member of the group was hard to figure — a youngish man dressed only in a shirt and slacks, no sports coat. He seemed terribly nervous; repeatedly he brought out a big white handkerchief and wiped his brow. It was hard to know what role he played.

The trial was a bench trial — no jury. Neither Legal Aid nor Justin Lambert could afford jury fees.

Fortunately, we'd drawn a decent judge, Lionel Carpenter. He was generally regarded as fair, if not a great intellect.

When the case of Strawberry Point Harbor Associates vs. Lambert was called, Justin and I went up to one of the two tables in the well of the court. D. B. Luther and the local lawyer moved up to the other.

"Mr. Gold, you may call your first witness," said Judge Carpenter.

D. B. Luther walked slowly to the stand, a scowl on his face.

Mr. Gold, my adversary whose name I now remembered, got Luther to testify that, one, Strawberry Point Harbor Associates owned a parcel of land in Richardson Bay; two, the defendant's houseboat, named the Owl, was on that parcel; three, he, D. B. Luther, had personally served a thirty-day notice to vacate on Mr. Lambert and the Owl; and four, more than thirty days had elapsed since the service of the notice and Mr. Lambert was still there.

That was all D. B. Luther testified to. No testimony whatsoever pertaining to the existence of a landlord-tenant relationship.

I declined the opportunity to cross-examine. D. B. Luther returned to his seat at the table. Judge Carpenter asked Mr. Gold if he had any more witnesses. Mr. Gold said no. Plaintiff rested.

Judge Carpenter said, "Mr. Spenser, you may proceed."

I rose. "Your honor, I make a motion to dismiss the complaint based on the fact plaintiff has failed to prove the existence of a landlord-tenant relationship between Strawberry Point Harbor Associates and Mr. Lambert, which is of course the basic jurisdictional requirement for an unlawful detainer. The complaint reads, and this is paragraph three I'm quoting from, 'On or about November 1, 1972, plaintiff and defendant entered into an agreement for the rental of a parcel of real property approximately forty feet by thirty feet located at Gate Five, Waldo Point, County of Marin.' Plaintiff failed to put on any evidence whatsoever that this allegation is true.

"Plaintiff is the moving party, your honor. They have the burden of proof as to each and every allegation in the complaint. And in this case, they've failed to prove the single most important allegation."

I expected a long pause while Judge Carpenter pondered this unusual argument, but instead he immediately said, "I noticed that myself. Mr. Gold, everybody who tries unlawful detainers follows the same script, so to speak, but just now you didn't. And I'm not sure why. But in any event, to this point you haven't proven a case for unlawful detainer.

"However, it may have been just a memory lapse, so in the interests of justice, I'll let you reopen your case-in-chief to present evidence of a landlord-tenant relationship. But please get on with it."

I was so nervous I could barely breathe. But D. B. Luther and Mr. Gold seemed in worse shape. They were

71

angrily whispering to each other at their table. The scowl on Luther's face had intensified, and I thought I detected him shaking his head and saying no.

"Mr. Gold," said Judge Carpenter, "either proceed, or I'm going to dismiss the case."

"Your honor, if I may have just a minute to confer with my client. We may be able to simplify things here."

"Mr. Gold, the time to prepare a case is the day before in your office, not in the middle of trial. I've got four other trials stacked up behind you. I've already given you the benefit of the doubt once today, letting you reopen your case-in-chief. How many favors are you going to be asking for today?'

"Your honor, I very much need to talk to my client. I can't do anything at this point without that."

Poor Gold, I thought.

"All right," said Judge Carpenter. "I'll give you sixty seconds to confer. Your sixty seconds start now."

Gold raced back to the audience section to confer with the Wilkes Bashford suit guy and the guy in just a shirt and slacks. Gold was shaking his head no. Mr. Wilkes Bashford looked angry. The shirt guy looked nervous and distraught; he brought out his big white handkerchief and again wiped his brow. I started to smell blood in the water.

Just as the sixty seconds were up, Mr. Gold returned, stood in front of the judge, and said. "Your honor, we move to dismiss the complaint."

We'd won.

A roar erupted behind me. The voice of Waldo Point.

Judge Carpenter was furious. He banged his gavel and demanded order. But it didn't matter; the twenty or so Waldo Point residents were streaming out of the courtroom preparing to celebrate.

In the corridor outside the courtroom everyone started hugging each other. I hugged Justin, Asha, Kevin, Montse, and finally came to Becky. We embraced each other tightly. Then she lifted her hand, ran her fingers lightly through my hair, smiled seductively, and said in her low, sexy voice, "We're sooo lucky to have you on our team."

I felt a tingle. But exactly what did Becky's flirting mean?

A sudden worry seized me; I looked around to see where Kevin was. He was celebrating with a group of other people, his back turned to Becky and me.

Someone shouted, "Let's go to Achille's place and tell him." Immediately everyone scattered to the parking lot. Deserving time off from the office to celebrate victory in an important case, I too headed off to Achille's.

Half an hour later we were all trooping over the long gangway that crossed primordial ooze and the rotting deck of the ferryboat *San Rafael*, then climbing the steep, dark rickety staircase that led to Achille's peculiar residence.

The room was as before — sloped, smoky, crowded with people. But this time the room's smokiness included, in addition to cigarettes and Achille's sweet pipe tobacco, a generous contribution of marijuana. Many people were drinking beer.

Achille was seated in the same spot, against the wall on the uphill side, in front of his bookcases, pipe in hand, table on one side, floor lamp on the other. I didn't see his youthful paramour.

I pushed my way uphill through the crowd to greet him. Remaining seated, he held out both hands. "Rick Spenser, you brought us good fortune, which we sorely needed. We thank you so much."

I held his hands and smiled. "But you also ought to thank D. B. Luther. It was his unwillingness to lie that made it an easy victory."

"He has other bad traits, I assure you."

Someone shoved a beer into my hand, and all of us standing around Achille — Becky, Kevin, Hank, Montse, Justin, Asha and myself — toasted our legal victory. Achille's redheaded girlfriend appeared, bearing ice cream in paper cups. She distributed the ice cream, then sat on the arm of Achille's chair, leaning against him.

Since all the main actors were present, I thought it might be a good time to prod the clients' thinking forward a bit. "Had you thought," I said, "that now might be a good time to contact Strawberry Point Harbor Associates and see exactly how set they are with their present plans? Start some preliminary negotiations, in other words.

"Look at it this way. You're in a strong position right now, in that you won the first battle in court. You may not always have that advantage. There may be other battles, and you may not win those. I certainly can't guarantee a win every time we go into court. And don't ever say I did.

"And ultimately this whole thing has to be settled by negotiations, not litigation. You can't expect a judge to figure out how to resolve this very complex, very difficult situation. I think that to solve this thing, you have to get down to a detailed, almost boat-by-boat plan for reorganizing Waldo Point. And a judge can't do that. He doesn't have the time; he doesn't have the expertise.

"That's not to say litigation is useless. Litigation can be used to gain leverage, which we did today. And it can be used to slow things down, throw sand in the gears, which we also did today. But litigation can't *solve* the problem of Waldo Point. To do that, you need negotiations. And maybe the best time to explore talking to Strawberry Point Harbor Associates is now, when you have some leverage."

Everyone looked at the floor. I'd brought up a difficult subject.

At last Achille spoke. "I'm opposed to any negotiations with that group. They're a bunch of capitalist thieves who don't have any ties to this community and don't care about this community. All they're interested in is money and how to get rid of us. They'll never go along with anything we want, since we can't pay them as much as the plutocrats they're planning on selling their new berths to.

"Furthermore, I consider that Strawberry group totally dishonest, and I worry that we, who are poor, honest folk, would be bamboozled and stripped of everything we own if we ever got into negotiations with them. That, in any event, is my opinion." He put his pipe back in his mouth and pulled his shawl up around his shoulders.

Not exactly the response I was hoping for. And I'd noticed Hank vigorously nodding his head in full agreement with Achille.

Everyone in the circle around Achille remained silent, while behind us dozens of less politically interested houseboaters partied and celebrated.

At long last Becky spoke up. Looking fresh and sunny, even in the smoky, moldy environment of Achille's room. "I agree that in the end this whole mess can only be solved through negotiations. And Rick, I understand the distinction you make between what lawsuits are good for and what negotiations can do.

"But the problem is, SOW isn't ready to negotiate. We just started getting organized two months ago. We don't really know each other. We've conduced a census, but we're still adding up the totals.

"I can't go to a meeting with Strawberry Point Harbor Associates and say, 'Hi, my name is Becky Yates, and I represent the 200 people who live at Waldo Point.' I don't know who all those people are. And even among the people I do know, I don't know what they want or what they expect. As a matter of fact," — she pointed to herself — "I don't even know what *I* want.

"Now I agree with you, Rick, that at some point it's probably going to come down to drawing up a detailed plan showing how everything that wants to be here can fit into this limited space. But SOW isn't in a position to propose anything like that now. It's way too early.

"So in the end what I'm saying is, yes, we need to think about negotiations, like you say. But no, now is not the time to start them."

The discussion I'd initiated had not gone entirely the way I wanted. But at least I could take consolation from one fact confirmed. Not only was Becky glamorous and something of a flirt, she was also an intelligent, thoughtful leader.

10
GORDON ONSLOW FORD

"Do you know who Gordon Onslow Ford is?" Tiffany asked me soon after I began working with the Waldo Point houseboat community.

"No. Should I?"

"He's actually fairly famous. Famous in the art world, at least. He was one of the original Surrealists, part of the group in Paris in the 1930s that included André Breton, Yves Tanguy and Max Ernst. The reason I bring him up is that in his later years he lived on a houseboat in Sausalito."

"Really? Do you know where?"

"They say it was in Sausalito, but I don't know exactly where. He co-owned a boat with some poet, and apparently the two of them turned this houseboat into a sort of salon for Bay Area artists in the 40s and 50s."

"Have you seen any of Ford's work?"

"I have. A gallery on the floor above us reps him. I know one of the partners there, and she's shown me what they have. She's also the one who told me about Onslow Ford living on a houseboat. By the way, he's referred to as Onslow Ford, not just Ford. Apparently it's a double last name."

"What do you think of his work?"

"It's trippy. Definitely surrealistic. You should take a look sometime. I can set it up."

Two weeks later Tiffany and I were driving to San Francisco for my introduction to the artwork of Gordon Onslow Ford.

The Engelhart Gallery looked like all the other galleries in the big white building on Geary Street — high ceilings, white walls, polished concrete floors, spot lighting. Tiffany's friend Elizabeth, an older woman with short, frosted hair and an elegant manner, graciously brought out all her gallery's Onslow Fords.

Looking at the paintings was like being catapulted into outer space. Twinkling stars, strange amoeba-like forms, spirals, hieroglyphics — all floated in what seemed like three-dimensional space, weightless, timeless. Some of the paintings featured vivid colors — intense oranges, greens and blues. Others were entirely black and white.

In a colorful example, multi-colored circles within circles could be taken as the top of a snail, the top of a covered vase, or an eyeball, while beside the circles strange squirrel-like animals climbed shafts of light.

In a black-and-white work, dense patterns of intersecting white lines and clouds evoked the glowing trails and explosions of light produced in particle accelerators.

"I'm impressed," I said. "These are amazing,"

"I agree," Elizabeth said. "Gordon is greatly underrated. That's why we're so happy to represent him."

"Tiffany says he lived on a houseboat in Sausalito."

"That's not exactly true. Gordon co-owned a boat, the *Vallejo,* along with Jean Varda, who was a French poet. Varda lived on the boat, but Gordon didn't. Instead, Gordon used his half of the boat as his studio. But of course Gordon was very much a part of what made the *Vallejo* a special place in the late 40s and 50s."

"It was a special place?"

"Oh yes, a haven for artists and writers. A lot of well-known people spent time on the *Vallejo*. Henry Miller and Alan Watts. Some of the Beat Generation writers — Jack Kerouac and Gary Snyder. Roberto Matta and Wolfgang Paalen, who were painters Gordon first met in the 1930s, when they were all part of the Surrealist movement in Paris. Harry Partsch, the composer, and Hodo Tobase, a Japanese calligrapher with whom Gordon studied."

"When was all this?"

"Gordon and Jean Varda bought the *Vallejo* in 1947. Gordon moved out and gave his half to Alan Watts in 1958."

All this surprised me. I was completely unaware the Richardson Bay waterfront had once been considered an artists' haven. The only waterfront history I'd heard about revolved around two shipyards — the World War II Marinship and Donlon Arques's eccentric enterprise.

"Is Gordon still alive?" I asked,

"Yes. He lives in Inverness and still paints."

"How old is he?"

"He's sixty-four. He was quite young when he was in Paris."

"And what about the *Vallejo*? Is it still around?"

"Yes. It's an old ferryboat, you know."

An old ferryboat. Like the *San Rafael* and the *Charles Van Damme*. Was the *Vallejo* as decrepit as they were?

I asked Elizabeth if she knew exactly where the *Vallejo* was located. She did, having visited it. Noticing my curiosity, she offered to show me on a map.

The *Vallejo* was moored at the end of a tiny one-block road called Varda Landing, located in Sausalito, but at the town's northernmost edge, just south of Waldo Point.

"Are you game to drop by the *Vallejo* on our way back?" I asked Tiffany.

"Sure."

Driving back to Marin County I asked myself: Did today's Waldo Point have any claim to being a haven for artists and writers? Didn't seem like it did.

Justin Lambert had said on his application form that he was a sculptor, but I hadn't seen any evidence of sculpting when I visited him on the Owl. Chris Roberts, the boat sculptor, apparently no longer lived at Waldo Point. And no one else I'd met there had even identified as an artist or a writer. I'd seen paintings on the sides of houseboats, but with their intense colors and swirling Art Nouveau-esque forms, they all seemed derivative of the rock-concert poster art that had been the rage in San Francisco a decade earlier. Not exactly cutting edge.

Did the current residents of Waldo Point even know about the waterfront's artistic and literary heritage? For example, if I mentioned the name "Gordon Onslow Ford" to Becky and Kevin, would they know who I was talking about? Probably not. After all, they hadn't arrived in Waldo Point until the early 70s, a decade and a half after Onslow Ford had decamped to West Marin.

From Bridgeway, Sausalito's main drag, a short drive through an area filled with warehouses, storage facilities and dingbat apartment buildings took Tiffany and me to Varda Landing. After curving around a small cove in which four or five small houseboats floated, the road ended at a spit of land. At the end of the spit sprawled a collapsing behemoth that had to be the *Vallejo*.

Time had not been kind to the *Vallejo*. All the paint had peeled off, and the vessel's rotting carcass had turned a burnt-looking dark brown. The front deck had collapsed in the middle; weeds grew between the planks.

Even worse, over the years ugly excrescences had been added to the poor *Vallejo*. On top there now sat not only a proper pilothouse, but also several ungainly shacks. Lean-to sheds had taken over the side decks. The front had been turned into a checkerboard of blue-and-white squares.

Were they windows? They looked more like pieces of cheap, opaque plastic.

The other two retired ferryboats I'd seen, the *San Rafael* and the *Charles Van Damme*, had at least been allowed to die with dignity, still looking like ferryboats. The *Vallejo* had been denied even that privilege.

The air smelled of rot and dead fish. "A real junker," said Tiffany. A pigeon flew out from the *Vallejo's* interior.

Driving back to San Rafael, I felt depressed. Had I arrived on the scene long after the glory days of the Richardson Bay waterfront?

I'd recently read a magazine article that described the classic trajectory of a once-hot vacation destination. At first, the destination — it could be a Mediterranean fishing village, a Caribbean island, a ski resort in the Alps — is known only to a select few, the cognoscenti. At this early stage locals outnumber tourists by a wide margin, and the locals go about their business much as they always have.

Then, word about the destination starts to get out. More tourists begin to come, and more hotels open. Next, articles appear in all the major newspapers and travel magazines. Tourists flood in, and big chain hotels mushroom. Now there are more tourists than locals in town, all the locals work in the tourist industry, and the streets are lined with T-shirt shops. By the time you, the average tourist, get there, it's too late.

Had I arrived at the Richardson Bay waterfront too late? Were the multitudes of young people who migrated there in the late 60s and early 70s, mainly from the Haight-Ashbury, comparable to mass-market tourists who overrun and consequently ruin a once-exclusive vacation destination?

Perhaps best not to think about things like that.

11
TAKING THE LEAP

With the Owl case resolved, I finally had time to get to the tall stack of Waldo Point-related papers that had been accumulating in my office ever since Becky, Kevin and Hank first walked in.

Kevin brought in the final results of the census and survey SOW conducted, and I dove into that first. The census identified 185 households living at Waldo Point, representing 324 residents. I was surprised. This was substantially more than I'd been told only a month before. Twice as many, in fact.

Waldo Point was definitely a low-income community. Yearly income *per household* was:

Less than $3,500	47%
$3,500 – $4,999	17%
$5,000 – $9,999	16%
Over $10,000	20%

Waldo Point was also a very young community. Achille and Hank were exceptions. The exact age breakdown was:

Under 18	15%
18-29	43%
30-39	31%
Over 40	11%

As I suspected, many Waldo Point residents were recent arrivals. Only fifty-three percent of current residents had lived there longer than three years.

Finally, under the heading "Questioning the Faith," the survey found:

Do you believe in God?

Yes	64%
No	15%
Undecided	21%

Do you believe in Santa Claus?

Yes	54%
No	26%
Undecided	20%

The residents of Waldo Point were believers.

I turned to the permit for the redevelopment of Waldo Point, the one granted three years before by the County of Marin to Donlon Arques. Specifically, I perused its thirty-plus conditions.

Kevin had mentioned one of these conditions to me earlier. It provided that the permit would expire automatically if no work were performed for a continuous period of ninety days. Kevin claimed no work had been performed at all during the three years since the permit had been granted, let alone every ninety days.

This was an issue worth raising, but most likely not a winning issue. Strawberry Point Harbor Associates would probably be able to come up with someone willing to swear under penalty of perjury that every ninety days he had turned a shovel of dirt.

There was also an interesting condition Kevin hadn't mentioned. It read, "In the event permittee does not complete construction of at least one of the piers shown on Exhibit A by June 30, 1978, the county shall have the right, in its sole discretion, to revoke or modify this permit."

June 30, 1978 was by now only seven months away. And as far as I knew, Strawberry Point Harbor Associates hadn't even started meaningful construction.

Wasn't building a pier jutting out into the ocean and containing electrical, water and sewage lines a fairly complex enterprise? Wasn't seven months a fairly tight schedule?

The county had been turning away pleas for help from Waldo Point residents by saying the permit had already been granted, therefore Strawberry Point Harbor Associates had "vested rights," therefore there was nothing the county could do. But if Strawberry Point Harbor Associates did not complete construction of a least one pier by June 30, 1978, which certainly seemed possible, all these arguments vanished. The county could do anything it wanted. If SOW could muster enough political support, it could get the plan modified.

A few days later Kevin called to say the other two attorneys he'd talked about — the law professor from Golden Gate University and the Waldo Point resident who was also a lawyer — were definitely on board, and SOW wanted to arrange a meeting among the three of us to start putting together the much-anticipated big lawsuit against the county and Strawberry Point Harbor Associates. Was Legal Aid also definitely on board? I told Kevin I'd get back to him soon.

I went to Sam, my boss, showed him the results of the income survey and told him about the two other attorneys SOW had recruited. Sam agreed that both the conditions he'd established for Legal Aid's participation in a large-scale lawsuit had been met. He gave me the go-ahead and wished me good luck.

I was overjoyed. It was actually happening. My first big case, and on behalf of a fascinating client.

What I didn't realize was that I was a step closer to the dark parking lot and the murderous truck.

12
ATTORNEYS' MEETING ON THE *SAN RAFAEL*

SOW wanted the initial meeting of the three attorneys to take place in public, in Achille's room, with members of SOW invited to attend and ask questions. I was leery of the idea, afraid such a meeting might degenerate into a free-for-all of bad ideas and unreasonable demands from spacey SOW members. But I didn't want to make an issue of SOW's commitment to participatory democracy, so in the end I agreed.

We three attorneys met in the Waldo Point parking lot. It wasn't hard to tell who was the law professor and who was the Waldo Point resident.

Bruce Krieger had the stereotypical law-professor look. Slight and spindly of frame, with thinning hair and a stoop, he wore glasses, a tweed spots coat and a tie. Worry clouded his face as he looked around the parking lot. Worry turned to horror as his eyes alighted upon the rotting hulk of the *Charles Van Damme*. He looked to be in his forties.

Dan Porter, on the other hand, had the big, brawny frame, thick mop of unruly blond hair, and sunburnt, outdoorsy look generic among the men of Waldo Point. He wore a plaid flannel shirt and jeans, could have been anywhere between twenty-five and forty, and looked completely at ease in the Waldo Point parking lot. He just didn't look like a lawyer.

We headed down the dirt road toward Gate Five and Achille's abode. As we were walking, Professor Krieger whispered to me, "I don't know how I let myself get roped into this."

The sight of the derelict *San Rafael* and the precarious gangway that led into it sent the good professor into a panic. I could sympathize. The first time I'd been here, the long, high gangway with no railings had frightened me too. As a matter of fact, I still didn't like it, though after several visits I'd grown used to it.

We coaxed Professor Krieger along the gangway into the void space. The smell of rotting wood and polluted water enveloped us, and I could see his nose twitch in disgust. When we reached the steep, dark, rickety, tilted staircase that led to Achille's room, Krieger whispered to me, "I had no idea it would be this bad."

Achille's aerie was, as always, packed with people and smells. Achille was seated in his usual chair, covered by his usual shawl, with his usual pipe in hand, and his usual juvenile girlfriend by his side. The only change in the room was that an area to the right of Achille had been cleared to make way for three chairs. Seats for Professor Krieger, Dan Porter and myself.

The professor spoke first. "This is the one and only time I'm coming to Marin County on this matter. I'll write the environmental-law sections of the complaint and brief, but I won't come to any more client meetings, and I won't make any court appearances."

Silence ensued. A sense of deflated expectations filled the room.

I felt obligated to try to change the tone of the meeting. "How's the environmental-law argument shaping up?"

Krieger's scowl relaxed. "Not bad. It's actually fairly solid. Quite solid, in fact."

At least something.

I looked at Dan Porter. "What's your availability, Dan?" Somehow I'd become the moderator of the meeting.

"I don't have any problem attending more client meetings. I'd probably be there as a Waldo Point resident anyway. And I'm willing to appear in court. But I have to warn you, I don't have much courtroom experience. You'll have to take the lead in any court hearings."

This was perturbing. To begin with, I'd promised Sam there would be three rowers manning the oars of the big Waldo Point lawsuit. Now it appeared one oar — my oar — was much bigger than the other two.

Also, I wasn't that experienced myself. I'd only been in practice three years. If Dan Porter had virtually no courtroom experience, which he seemed to be implying, our team was severely lacking in that regard.

Before I could think of what to say next, Dan resumed talking. "I'd like to focus on developing the right-of-navigation argument. I've already been doing some research. Did you know the right of navigation traces back to Roman law? Under the Roman *jus navigandi*, the coasts of the sea were considered common property for purposes of fishing, drying nets and building huts related to fishing. The principle underlying the Roman right of navigation was that the sea is an element that belongs to all mankind, like the air, and — "

At this point, I tuned out. I might have been in practice for only three years, but at least I knew something about the judges of the Marin County Superior Court. They were former small-town lawyers who, over the years, had cultivated friends and political connections. They weren't legal scholars, and they certainly weren't interested in Roman law. If you cited a recent California Supreme Court or Court of Appeal case, they would probably follow it. Otherwise, they decided cases based on general ideas of justice and fairness.

On the other hand, if Dan Porter wanted to take full responsibility for developing the right-of-navigation argument, that was fine with me. I'd lost faith in the argument; I didn't see it leading to any positive result. Dan's written contribution would probably be long and verbose, but even that could be seen as a positive. It would add weight and bulk to our moving papers.

When Dan paused for a breath, I interrupted. "That sounds great, Dan. You are hereby appointed our man in charge of the right-of-navigation argument. Good luck with it. Now let me see, what other arguments do we have?

"There's the no-construction-for-ninety-days argument," I said, answering my own question. "I can handle that. It's really just putting together a declaration. Kevin, do you want to be the declarant, the one who swears there hasn't been any construction activity?"

"Sure."

"Okay, I'll do up a draft and shoot it to you. Now, are there any more arguments we need to assign?"

I looked at Dan and Bruce. No response.

I wasn't eager to open the floor to the SOW membership. But given SOW's explicit instructions, there didn't seem to be any other choice.

I looked at the large crowd of SOW members crowded together in Achille's smoky, smelly room. Looked down on them to be precise, because we three lawyers were much higher than they were, both because we were seated in conventional chairs while most of them were either sitting on the floor or in beanbag chairs, and because we were seated uphill while they were downhill. Was this difference in height, which of course reflected the difference in status that exists whenever lawyers and laypersons interact, intentional? I wasn't sure.

"Anybody in the audience have any ideas about additional arguments we should include?"

To my surprise — and relief — no one said a word.

I surveyed the faces of the four people I recognized as SOW's leaders. Becky and Kevin were beaming. Their organizational skills were bearing fruit, their grand strategy moving ahead. Hank also looked happy. He had one entire attorney specializing his favorite right-of-navigation argument.

Only Achille was an enigma. Looking down, puffing on his pipe from time to time, he showed no emotion. I was surprised he hadn't said anything.

"Okay," I said. "Since the only task I have so far is putting together the no-construction-for-ninety-days argument, which isn't much, I'll have time to write the introduction and statement of facts."

This suited me perfectly. If a judge was going to read any part of our moving papers, which wasn't a given, he was going to read the introduction and statement of facts. After all, most cases were decided on the facts, not abstract legal principles. Our best chance of winning this case was by framing the facts in our favor.

The meeting's main business wrapped up, I took the opportunity to bring up the June 30, 1978 deadline for Strawberry Point Harbor Associates to complete construction of at least one pier. I pointed out that if the developer defaulted on the June 30, 1978 deadline, the entire "vested rights" problem would disappear, and the struggle would become purely political. The crowd seemed surprised at this news. And interested. More interested, in fact, than they had seemed during the discussion of the lawsuit.

With that, the meeting broke up. I left feeling relieved and satisfied. Everything was organized, everything was under control.

13
PILE DRIVER

My confidence that everything was under control lasted exactly five days. It took only a telephone call to shatter it.

The call came just as I walked into the office that morning. "Rick?" The voice of Kevin. "Any chance of your getting down here really fast. There's some heavy shit coming down."

"Heavy shit?"

"The Strawberries are trying to bring in a pile driver."

"Strawberries?"

"Strawberry Point Harbor Associates."

"And they're trying to bring in a . . ."

"Pile driver. To start building the first pier."

Strawberry Point Harbor Associates must have been thinking the same thing I was thinking. Seven months wasn't much time to build a complicated pier out into San Francisco Bay. They needed to get started now.

"You said heavy shit. I understand it's a blow the Strawberries have finally gotten their act together and started building their first pier. But why is it heavy shit?"

"It's chaos down here. Lots of people protesting. Some people have been moving boats in front of the pile driver. There're cops all around; they even have the sheriff's boat down here with cops on board, and there've been battles between those cops and houseboat people on skiffs. Lots of people have already been arrested. I don't know how many, but I've seen people being arrested and dragged away. Achille was here for a while, but then he collapsed. People think he may have suffered a heart attack. Man, it is *crazy* down here."

"Wow. That sounds awful. So sorry to hear it. . . . But as far as my coming down this morning, I'm not sure what that would accomplish. I don't have any influence over the Marin County Sheriff's Department. Unfortunately."

"Understood. But we need an attorney down here, if only to bear witness. We called Ray Alencar, and — damn it, wouldn't you know — he's out of town. So we'd really, really appreciate it if you could come."

Ray Alencar? The name was familiar; I'd seen it on courtroom calendars. He was apparently a fairly active Marin County attorney.

But why did the houseboaters call *him*? Call him before calling me, in fact? Were the houseboaters using an attorney I didn't know about? Did I have a competitor?

"Sure. I'll be down as soon as possible. Give me half an hour."

"Great. And while you're here, we can talk about the big lawsuit you and the other two attorneys are working on. We need that baby filed as soon as possible, so we can hopefully use it to stop this shit."

I cringed in embarrassment. The truth was, I hadn't even started my sections of the houseboaters' lawsuit. Working in a legal aid office, there was always something more immediate, more urgent, than working on a case with an indefinite deadline.

"Also," Kevin said, "if you come down here, you can see the huge number of people who care about this issue and how strongly they feel. It'll give you some motivation. Are you free?"

"Yes, I'm coming down."

The Waldo Point parking lot, usually so spacious, was that day sardine-packed with vehicles, many of them — at least twenty — cop cars and paddy wagons. I finally managed to find space on an embankment next to the lot.

The deafening, continuous shriek of a siren blanketed the area. In addition to the usual smells of sewage and seawater, an acrid, chemical smell fouled the air.

Emerging from the scrum of vehicles, my eyes landed on a group of people sitting on the ground, many crying and rubbing their faces with water-soaked towels. Becky was among them, though she herself didn't seem to be crying. Instead, she seemed to be helping other people.

"What's going on?" I asked a bystander.

"Fucking pigs are using mace."

My eyes started to tear up in sympathy, and my stomach felt nauseous. It may have been voyeurism, but I couldn't stop staring at the poor people trying to get the mace out of their eyes and off their skin.

"So what do you think about the cops using mace?" Kevin's voice from behind.

"Not good, not good."

"Want to take a look at the front lines?"

I sighed. "I guess."

We headed toward the water. "What's that horrible noise?" I asked.

"That's a siren on the *San Rafael*. We blow it whenever there's an emergency and we need everybody to show up."

"Have you heard anything more about Achille?"

"No, I haven't."

We ended up on a floating dock that had a full view of the channel where the action was taking place. The view resembled a wide-screen movie battle scene.

On the left, two burly sheriff's deputies had boarded a houseboat and were in the process of physically subduing a young man — grabbing him, throwing him to the floor of his boat.

"Why are they going after that guy?" I asked.

"That's Joel Kravis," Kevin said. "They need to move his boat to get the pile driver into position, and he's trying to stop them."

As we watched, the cops pinned Kravis to the floor, put their knees on him, and snapped handcuffs on his wrists.

Meanwhile, to the right, a Lilliputian naval battle raged. Cops in skiffs battled houseboaters in skiffs, each side using poles and oars to try to push the other away. The siren on the *San Rafael* continued to shriek.

Further out in the channel a large, powerful speedboat lay in wait. On its side were the words "COAST GUARD."

The Coast Guard!

"Why is the Coast Guard here? Has Congress declared war on Waldo Point?"

"I'll bet the sheriff talked the Coast Guard into providing logistical support. There were a couple of incidents in the past when the sheriff tried to come in here by water in order to serve abatement orders. And both times the sheriff's guys fell flat on their faces. Basically they had to turn their boats around and flee. So I suspect the sheriff figured that for his boys to compete on water, they needed better boats and better equipment. And somehow he managed to sweet-talk the Coast Guard into providing it."

"I don't see any pile driver. Where's the pile driver?"

"It's out there. See, to the left of the big Coast Guard boat."

With this guidance I was able locate, quite a distance away, the pile driver, which sat on a barge. Next to it floated a tugboat, waiting to pull the barge into the channel. But for the moment, nothing moved.

"Did you receive any notice they were going to bring in a pile driver today?"

"No. Absolutely none."

We watched the Battle of the Channel for five minutes. The cops sat Joel Kravis upright and began questioning him. The skiffs continued their jousting, neither side able to gain the upper hand.

I felt awful. For many reasons. The brutality of the cops and their military-style invasion disgusted me. The sheer amount of resources the county, and now even the United States government, were devoting toward eradicating the houseboat community appalled and worried me. My eyes still felt sympathetic pain from seeing the houseboaters who'd been maced. Most of all, I felt guilty.

Guilty because the Waldo Point houseboat community came to me hoping I could stop precisely this. And I hadn't done so. Indeed, to that point, I hadn't done a lick of work on the big lawsuit I'd so effusively promised.

"So, has this given you enough motivation?" Kevin must have had a degree in psychology.

I offered a grim smile. "I think we need to talk. But maybe we can find a place that's calmer and where the siren isn't so loud."

Kevin led me back to the shoreline. There he picked up Becky and Dan Porter, the attorney who lived nearby, and the four us moved to an area of the parking lot that enjoyed relative quiet. On the way, we learned that Achille had recovered and apparently *not* suffered a heart attack.

In the parking lot Kevin once again set the agenda. "Hey guys," he said, looking at Dan and me, "we need help, and we need it fast. We've got to get something in front of the courts to try to stop this madness. I know you're working on the lawsuit we talked about last Friday. The question now is how can we speed that lawsuit up and get in front of the courts as soon as possible?"

Dan and I looked at each other, neither of us wanting to say anything until we'd had time to think.

In legal terms, what Kevin was asking for was filing suit and immediately going for a TRO — temporary restraining order. This was theoretically possible. The problem was that neither Dan nor I — nor our missing colleague from Golden Gate University, I was sure — had thought much beyond the sizable task of putting together all the paperwork needed simply to get the damn suit filed. As for what came after that — going for a TRO or whatever — we hadn't had time to think about it.

Going for a TRO would require a whole new set of papers, above and beyond those needed to file suit. We'd have to put together more declarations, develop more legal arguments. All this was possible, but hadn't been budgeted for.

On the other hand, Kevin was clearly right in saying SOW needed help now, not four months from now. The houseboaters couldn't hold out against overwhelming military-style force for long. And the longer we waited, the more the new pier would edge toward becoming a *fait accompli,* which in turn would lower our chances for success in court. We were never going to stop a half-built project. Facts on the ground trumped arguments in a lawsuit.

"Sounds like the client wants and needs a TRO," I finally said to Dan.

"I agree. I think we've got our marching orders."

This was the first time I'd been lead attorney on a major case, and I soon realized the role, while prestigious, wasn't a barrel of monkeys. Instead, it was a jumble of telephone calls, negotiations, scheduling and rescheduling.

First order of business was to get ourselves — SOW's legal team — organized. Dan and I divided up the extra work needed for the TRO application, and I managed to persuade the professor to get his promised contribution in early. Dan and I would work over the weekend to have everything written by Monday morning. Legal Aid would bring in an extra secretary on Monday to help with the typing. If all went well, the entire package, including the TRO application, would be ready for filing late Monday.

The next order of business required, unfortunately, dealing with the county. Under the rules governing TRO applications, we were obligated give the county and the developer a reasonable opportunity to respond in writing to our moving papers. That meant negotiating some sort of schedule.

I worked through my contact in county counsel's office, Sheryl Harding. The county wanted two full days for itself and the developer to respond. If we got all our papers filed and served by the end of Monday, they would file and serve their responses by the end of Wednesday. We could all go in and see a judge on Thursday.

This left the embattled houseboaters more exposed than I wanted. Even after the weekend break there could be four more days of skirmishes, arrests and mace attacks. But the schedule was the best I could do, and in the end everyone agreed to it.

Dan Porter, whom I'd earlier pegged as dreamy and impractical, turned out to be a workhorse. Legal Aid's clerical staff performed as if their lives depended on it.

At 4:45 on Monday afternoon, I hopped into my Mustang, sped to the Civic Center, got to the clerk's office just before the five-o'clock filing deadline, filed all the papers, and then hand-delivered a conformed copy to county counsel's office. SOW had come up with a messenger who delivered another copy to Strawberry Point Harbor Associates' attorney in San Francisco. We did it.

I drove slowly home, picking up a pizza along the way. Then I collapsed.

14
DAY IN COURT

The Marin County Civic Center was Frank Lloyd Wright's last design and the only time a government building he designed was actually built. Idyllically set amidst rolling, undeveloped hills, with a lagoon to one side, the building complex has sand-beige walls, a sky-blue roof and a 172-foot-tall gold tower. The main facade features three tiers of arches, the size of the arches decreasing dramatically from bottom to top. This facade resembles, and was probably inspired by, a Roman aqueduct, the Pont de Gard, outside Nimes, France.

The interiors of the Civic Center, particularly the wing where the courts are housed, are not those of your typical courthouse. All courtrooms are round. Even outside the courtrooms, no right angles exist. Everything — every corner, every window opening — is rounded.

Wright's theory was that since courtrooms and their surroundings are places of conflict and strife, their architecture should strive to reduce tensions and foster tranquility and harmony. Architecture could do this, Wright believed, by avoiding sharp divisions, sharp corners and opposing walls, and by appearing as frictionless as possible. That, at least, was the theory.

As is well known, theory doesn't always work. I certainly didn't feel tranquil or harmonious that Thursday afternoon, standing uncomfortably inside the Civic Center in an interior hallway separating the courtroom of Judge Carl Daley from his private office.

For one thing, clashes had been occurring at Waldo Point the entire week. More people maced, more people arrested, more people dragged over dirt and gravel to police paddy wagons. Worst of all, the pile driver had managed to drive a few piles.

Late the previous afternoon I'd received the responses of the county and Strawberry Point Harbor Associates to our moving papers. The centerpiece was a declaration by the director of the county's Department of Public Works. It almost singed my hands as I read it.

Waldo Point, according to the director, represented "the worst fire, health and safety hazard in the county." He buttressed this generalization with numerous specifics, while declarations from other county department heads provided even more detail. It was scary stuff, even I had to admit.

The county and the developer barely addressed our legal arguments. They didn't try to refute them, they simply dismissed them with a wave. This case would be decided on the facts, our opponents were insisting, and the relevant facts were the threats that Waldo Point posed to public health and safety.

The hearing was to be held in Judge Daley's private office, no clients present, off the record. This was standard procedure for a TRO application.

Oddly, while I'd never appeared before Judge Daley in court, I'd met him socially. He was on Marin Legal Aid's board of directors. We'd said friendly hellos a few times — at Legal Aid Christmas parties, bar events — but we'd never had a meaningful conversation. He had a reputation for being fair and intelligent, and I felt we'd been lucky drawing him as our judge.

Dan Porter and I had left a score of SOW members, some bruised and bandaged, most looking very tired, outside in the public corridor as a clerk ushered us into the private hallway behind the courtrooms. Once inside we learned we were the first of the three parties to arrive. The clerk asked us to stand in the hallway.

Soon another man arrived — the same man I'd seen at the trial of the Owl, the man I'd dubbed Mr. Wilkes Bashford for his fancy clothes. He sized up Dan and me with a condescending look, then introduced himself as Lloyd Morgan, attorney for Strawberry Point Harbor Associates. I'd guessed right at the trial of the Owl. After a chilly handshake and exchange of cards with each of us, Morgan moved away and stood with his back to the wall. I looked at his card. His offices were in Three Embarcadero Center, one of downtown San Francisco's most prestigious office towers.

Seeing Morgan's spiffy outfit impelled me to look down at my own clothes. My suit was okay, but the shoes were pathetic — scuffed brown lace-ups. I glanced over at Lloyd Morgan's gleaming black loafers. I really needed to buy a new pair of dress shoes.

Last to arrive was the redoubtable Ken Riciarelli, Marin County Counsel, with my supposed friend Sheryl Harding walking behind and carrying all the files. Sheryl's role seemed to be that of slave girl.

Riciarelli was a big man, both bulky and tall, with a mass of curly salt-and-pepper hair and a classic bronzed Italian face. He shook hands hurriedly with Dan and me, waved to Lloyd Morgan, and immediately barged into the clerk's office to inform her that all parties were present and we were ready to start. He was obviously a take-charge kind of guy.

Soon the door to Judge Daley's private office opened, and the five of us — Dan and I for SOW, Riciarelli and Sheryl for the county, and Lloyd Morgan for the developer — marched in. To my great pleasure, Judge Daley greeted me as "Rick."

Once inside, I looked around. The spacious wood-paneled office was round, the tall built-in bookcases bearing pristine sets of Official Reports were curved, and even the judge's Texas-sized desk was round. Five round-backed guest chairs had been brought in, and they were arranged in — what else? — a semi-circle.

Judge Daley looked exactly like a judge should look. His elegantly combed-back silver hair complemented his flowing black robe. His chiseled features and strong jaw suggested that, in his youth, he'd been a lady-killer.

He began by saying, "Gentlemen, and Ms. Harding, I've read all your filings, you don't need to repeat yourselves. But I'm sure each of you wants a few minutes to speak, so we'll begin with the moving party, Save Our Waterfront. Which of you" — he looked at Dan and me — "wants to speak for Save Our Waterfront?"

By prearrangement with Dan, I held up my hand.

"Go ahead, Mr. Spenser."

I proceeded to expound what I regarded as our best fact-based argument, the same argument I'd emphasized in writing the introductions and statements of facts in our moving papers.

The permit for the redevelopment of Waldo Point had been issued three years ago. Since then, almost everything had changed. Then, the owner had been Donlon Arques, long a member of the community, known to everyone, a friend to many. Now the owner was a mysterious development group out of San Francisco, with no ties to the community, known to no one. Three years ago, assurances had been made that no one would be displaced. Now, Strawberry Point Harbor Associates was making no bones about the fact everyone now living at Waldo Point would have to go. The developer's plans threatened the displacement of more than three hundred individuals, yet this fact had never even been considered in the planning process that led to the 1974 permit.

It was time to pause, step back and reconsider the entire project. Not only was this good public policy, it was also — and here I tried to tie our factual argument to our best legal argument — exactly what was required by the California Environment Quality Act.

When I finished, Judge Daley showed no reaction. Instead, he simply said, "Mr. Riciarelli, you want to go next?"

Ken Riciarelli's presentation revolved around ten words: "the worst fire, health and safety hazard in the county." He must have repeated those ten words at least a dozen times. Looking at Waldo Point, he saw nothing but squalor. He spoke rapidly, vehemently. He didn't even mention any of our legal arguments.

Last to speak was Lloyd Morgan. He seconded everything Riciarelli had said, adding that Strawberry Point Harbor Associates was absolutely committed to wiping out every last fire, health and safety hazard that now existed or ever would exist at Waldo Point. He also emphasized his client had a very large monthly carrying cost for the property, and would suffer severe financial harm if any TRO or injunction were granted.

After Morgan had finished, Judge Daley remained silent for a full minute, resting his chin on his hand, his elbow on the arm of his chair. Despite the roundness of the room, the roundness of the judge's desk, the roundness of my chair, I felt gripped by anxiety. Thanks for nothing, Frank Lloyd Wright.

Finally the judge said, "Mr. Spenser, Mr. Porter, the dilemma I have with your application — "

Everything within me shriveled. This was not starting off well.

" — is this. Let's suppose I grant you a TRO, and later on perhaps an injunction. And then, shortly after that, there's a fire at Waldo Point that kills ten people. Or an epidemic breaks out, and it infects ninety and kills three.

"How could I live with myself after that? And I'm not talking about the fact I'd be run out of office, or at the very least defeated in the next election, as I would deserve to be. I'm taking about my own conscience. How could I live with myself, knowing I'd let a dangerous situation run on, and that situation had resulted in ten deaths, or three deaths, or whatever. I'd feel I was personally responsible for those deaths, and it would haunt me to my grave.

"So it is with these thoughts foremost in my mind that I'm going to deny the application for a TRO. I do worry about the three hundred plus individuals who, as things stand now, are going to be losing their homes. I wish there could be some modification of the plans so that at least some of these people could be accommodated, and I encourage you, Mr. Riciarelli and Mr. Morgan, to think in that direction. But as far as stopping, even if only temporarily, a project that's specifically designed to ameliorate what appear to be extremely unsafe and dangerous conditions, I simply can't do that."

I had to force myself to breathe. Acid gushed into my stomach; a sharp pain drilled into my forehead.

I'd failed. Failed myself, failed the Waldo Point community, failed all the people who'd been arrested or maced, failed Sam my boss who'd backed me up — failed everyone. This was the first time in my career I'd been number one attorney on a major case. And it was a total defeat.

"Thank you, gentlemen, and Ms. Harding," Judge Daley was saying as everyone packed up and began filing out. I forced my half-paralyzed muscles to do the same. Ken

Riciarelli and Lloyd Morgan completely ignored Dan and me as we all exited. Sheryl Harding rolled her eyes at me as if to say, "I told you so."

Out in the public corridor, I took on the responsibility of breaking the bad news to the twenty or so SOW members who'd been waiting all the time. When I'd finished, Becky and Kevin embraced each other and rested their heads on each other's shoulder, eyes closed. Hank cursed loudly and stalked away. Everyone else expressed dejection in his or her own way.

"We need to go and tell Achille," a voice said.

I started to say I needed to get back to the office and didn't have time to go to Achille's. To be honest, I wanted to slip offstage and disappear out the back of the theater. But then I thought I'd had plenty of time to go to Achille's and receive the plaudits of the crowd after I'd won the Owl case. Shouldn't I man up and face the crowd after losing this case?

Achille's sloping lair smelled worse than ever, a putrid blend of rotting wood, ocean muck, stale cigarette smoke and sickly-sweet pipe-tobacco smoke. The thirty or so people present all exuded misery. Hank paced around the space cursing.

When I talked to Achille, though, he didn't seem disappointed. "I didn't expect anything else," he said. "The courts are instruments of the capitalist state, and they protect the interests of the capitalist class. You can't expect justice from them. Certainly not for people like us."

I couldn't help thinking back to a month earlier, when I'd come here after my victory in the Owl case. Then I'd been the waterfront's hero, the center of attention, their savior. How things had changed.

In fact, I had the feeling people were now avoiding me. A group had coalesced and was avidly discussing something. But their body language made clear I was not welcome to the discussion.

I hadn't expected SOW to dismiss me so quickly and abruptly. After all, hadn't I warned them we weren't going to win every time we went to court?

But fame and glory are fleeting, I reminded myself. My career as the houseboaters' go-to lawyer had been fun while it lasted, but nothing is forever.

I left Achille's fetid headquarters feeling even more depressed than I'd felt leaving Judge Daley's round office.

15
SURPRISE!

The first winter storm of the season slammed into the Bay Area that December night, howling winds and driving rain in tow. The windows of my flimsy stucco apartment building rattled, the building itself shuddered. Whether because of the storm or because of the ignominious defeat I'd suffered earlier that day, I couldn't sleep. I tossed and turned all night, images of loss and devastation tramping through my mind.

Yet despite my insomnia, I somehow managed to sleep through the alarm. And once awake, I felt so lethargic and unmotivated I couldn't make up the time. As a result, I arrived at the office half an hour late.

Our receptionist Ruby greeted me with, "There's an urgent message for you."

I picked up the blue-and-white slip. It read: "Want to put a smile on your face? Come on down to Waldo Point ASAP. Kevin & the Gang."

What the hell? How could Kevin be so flippant when just a day before we'd suffered a devastating defeat, with no promise of better times in the future?

I had a client coming in that morning for a meeting about her unemployment-insurance appeal. But managing to catch her before she left home, I rearranged the appointment for later in the day. Then, brimming with curiosity but also apprehension, I dashed down Highway 101 to Waldo Point. Fortunately, the rains had gone away.

Upon arrival I saw a large knot of people bundled up in blankets or heavy parkas, their faces covered with mud and sweat, their hair matted. Improbably, given that it was ten in the morning, most seemed to be drinking beer. As I drew closer, the scent of pot wafted.

I saw Becky and Kevin in the group. Becky was wrapped in a Navajo blanket, chocolate-brown flecks of mud decorating her tan cheeks, water having turned her wavy golden locks straight. Kevin had a beer in one hand and a bandage on the other.

"What's going on? I asked.

"Come take a look," Kevin said.

He and Becky led me to the floating dock where, a week and a half earlier, I'd witnessed battles between houseboaters and cops. Several houseboats that had been there then were now gone — moved, presumably, by the cops — and in their place was the notorious pile diver. It was a silly-looking thing, a piece of equipment obviously designed for use on land — its huge rubber tires made that plain — rolled onto a small concrete barge. In front of the pile driver, three pairs of pilings poked out of the water. Next to it, a small tugboat floated idly.

But the pile driver held my attention for only a moment, for immediately behind it loomed something much larger. And more striking.

It was another rectangular concrete barge, like the one on which the pile driver sat, except this barge was much, much larger. At least a hundred feet in length. On top of it sat a one-story wood building painted barn red.

I looked more closely at the larger barge. Was I seeing correctly? I shut and reopened my eyes to make sure.

Yes, I was seeing correctly. The huge barge with the red building on top was *sunk*. It rested on the mud bottom. Like the Owl.

But that wasn't the most shocking thing. The most shocking thing was that the huge barge appeared to have been *deliberately* sunk. Numerous jagged holes punctuated its hull.

Suddenly all the pieces fit together, and a chill ran up my spine. The pile driver was in a cove. The huge concrete barge blocked the only entrance to the cove. Or exit from the cove. And because it was sunk, the barge couldn't be moved.

The pile driver was trapped! And not by accident, rather by deliberate —

I stopped myself just short of the word "sabotage."

What had I become part of? I was a lawyer, an officer of the court, an upholder of the rule of law. What had my clients done?

On the other hand, I had to admire their ingenuity.

I turned slowly to Becky and Kevin. "Is this what I think it is?"

They both broke out laughing.

"Seriously, is that big thing sunk?"

"It most definitely is," Becky said, in her most alluring low, smoky voice.

"I guess I'd better not ask if it was deliberately sunk."

Again they both laughed. "You didn't hear us talking about this yesterday at Achille's, did you?" Kevin asked.

"About this? No."

"Good. We were trying to make sure you didn't hear anything. We didn't want your fingerprints on this particular project."

I felt a warm glow. I'd been worried the houseboaters were rejecting me. Turned out they were simply protecting me.

"Wasn't last night a pretty lousy time to be outside in the elements all night, what with the wind and the rain and everything?"

"Here's my souvenir of the night," Kevin said, raising his bandaged hand.

"It was absolutely awful, miserable, terrible, cold, wet and everything else bad," said Becky. "It was also sort of fun." She tightened her Navajo blanket around herself.

Pointing to the enormous sunken barge I asked, "Where did this thing come from?"

"It was up in an area called Gate Six and a Half," Kevin answered. "It's north of here, very much out of the way. Hardly anybody knows about it. The barge is called the Red Barge, by the way."

"Does somebody own the Red Barge?"

"Yes. Guy named Billy the Kid."

"Billy the Kid?"

Kevin laughed. "That's not his real name, of course. His real name is Bill Kirk. But everybody calls him Billy the Kid. He calls himself Billy the Kid. He's right over there, where we first met up. Want to meet him?"

"Sure. But first, it would be possible to refloat the Red Barge, wouldn't it?"

"Of course."

"What would that entail?"

"You'd have to repair and seal all the holes. Then pump all the water out."

"How long would that take?"

He thought for a moment. "Probably six weeks to a couple of months. *If* you had easy access and the cooperation of the neighborhood. But if it's the Strawberries doing it, I'm not sure they'd have either of those things." Kevin smiled maliciously.

"Okay, then, what are the odds the Strawberries, as you call them, can complete the pier they're trying to build by June 30 of next year?"

"Damn close to zero, I'd say."

"Interesting. Very interesting."

As an officer of the court, I couldn't exactly condone what the houseboaters had done. But I had to admit, their lawless action had improved our legal position. We no longer had to worry about the vested rights issue.

On the way back, we saw three cops conferring with two civilians. I recognized the two civilians. One was Lloyd Morgan, the developer's attorney, aka Mr. Wilkes Bashford. The other was the man I'd seen with Morgan at the trial of the Owl, the man who that day wore only a shirt and slacks and seemed terribly nervous. Today, a cold December day, he wore a casual jacket over his shirt and still looked nervous. My hunch was that, despite his unsure appearance, he was actually the top officer or managing partner of Strawberry Point Harbor Associates.

Morgan, anger contorting his face, seemed to be lecturing and pointing his finger at the cops. The man in the casual jacket had his handkerchief out, ready for a wipe of the brow.

Morgan noticed me and immediately headed in my direction. The previous night's heavy rains had turned the ground to glutinous mud, and I couldn't help noticing, with a degree of *schadenfreude*, that Morgan was getting mud all over his black Italian suede loafers.

"Was this your idea?" he yelled at me when he arrived.

"What?"

"That thing that's sunk on our property. Was that your idea?"

Startled by his hostility, I was momentarily speechless. "That's really insulting," I finally said.

He remained silent, his eyes shooting daggers at me. After ten seconds or so, he said, "I'll just say this. If I come across any evidence indicating you were part of this vandalism, I won't have any hesitation reporting you to the State Bar."

He stalked away, getting even more mud on his Italian suede loafers.

"What a jerk." The voice of Kevin.

"You noticed, but on the other hand, maybe I shouldn't go over and hug Billy the Kid right at this minute."

"Um, probably not."

Montse swept into our group, bracelets and necklaces jangling. She obviously had not been up all night moving and sinking the Red Barge, for she looked well rested, clean and well groomed.

"Are you coming to our party, Rick?" she asked.

"What party?"

She turned to Becky and Kevin. "You mean you haven't invited him?"

"We were just getting around to it," answered Becky, sheepishly.

Montse turned back to me. "You *have* to come to our party. Tomorrow night, Saturday night. Starts at eight and goes on until the last person passes out."

"Where's it going to be?"

"On the Red Barge, where else?"

"The Red Barge? There's space for a party on the Red Barge?"

"Actually it works quite well," Kevin said. "The building on top's mainly just one big room. You'll see."

"Do you have an old lady?" Montse asked me. "Girlfriend? Wife? I'll bet you do, Mr. Rick Spenser, you handsome devil." She winked and swayed her hips toward me.

I hesitated.

But why? Did I honesty think I had a snowball's chance in hell of connecting with Becky, given that, number one, she was in a live-in relationship with Kevin, and number two, she was a client, and therefore off limits. Ridiculous.

"Yes," I replied.

"Then invite her. No, don't invite her, tell her she *has* to come. The party won't be complete without her."

I wasn't sure how Tiffany would respond to an invitation to spend Saturday night at Waldo Point. She generally preferred the elegant, the sophisticated. But when I got back to the office and called her at her gallery, she accepted immediately. "That sounds *so* exciting. I can't wait."

"Great. The houseboaters will be very pleased. And so will I."

"Do you remember that quote from *Heart of Darkness*? The one about Kurtz holding 'midnight dances with unspeakable rites.' Do you think at this party we'll see some midnight dances with unspeakable rites?"

"Tiff, honey, I'm doing the best I can."

16
PARTY TIME

By Saturday night the Red Barge had been renamed. Draped across the vessel's length was an enormous white banner reading, in bold black letters, "MIDNIGHT TRO."

I cringed the moment I saw the banner. Talk about contempt of court. What if Lloyd Morgan, the nasty attorney for Strawberry Point Harbor Associates, saw me heading into a party beneath this banner? He'd have me in front of the State Bar Court in minutes. As far as that went, what if Judge Carl Daily, who was on Marin Legal Aid's board of directors, learned I was partying under this middle finger raised to his ruling and his authority? He'd probably have enough pull to get me fired.

No sooner had I recovered from this shock than another appeared. The only way to get aboard the Midnight TRO was via a wood plank, completely without railings, that was barely a foot wide and at least ten feet long. I'd warned Tiffany not to wear high heels, but still I was afraid she'd want to turn around and go home without even going on board. Fortunately, she steeled herself and threaded her way across. Figuring that if Tiffany could do it, so could I, I somehow managed to follow.

We stepped through the door of the barn-red wood building. The air smelled like a brushfire at a pot plantation combined with a burst pipe at a brewery. Everything was bathed in orange light. A five-piece band wailed, while everyone else tried to shout above the music. People were packed shoulder to shoulder.

And there was hair. Hair everywhere, big hair, untamed, unrestrained, uncut, as much on the men (counting their beards) as on the women. And the bulk of this hair was so frizzy the entire room seemed enveloped in a crinkly scrim. I felt like a skinhead, even though my hair was considerably longer than when I was in high school in Pasadena. At least I wasn't alone: Tiffany's long but sleekly groomed black coif looked equally out of place.

Tiffany tugged at my sleeve and brought her mouth to my ear. "This party is really white," she shouted.

I looked around. Then I brought my mouth to her ear, cupped my hands around, and shouted, "What do you expect? It's Marin County. At least it's Marin County hippie."

Becky and Kevin materialized from out of the crowd. Becky wore a short leopard-print coat worn wide open, and beneath that only — repeat, only — a black lace brassiere. Lower down, she sported leopard-print hot pants and gold high-heel sandals. I could barely breathe.

When I finally wrested my attention away from Becky, I realized Kevin was saying something, but I couldn't hear him because of the noise. He and Becky set off and motioned us to follow. We ended up at ice chests full of beer and tables full of wine. I grabbed a beer, Tiffany a plastic cup of wine.

People started coming up to me, shaking my hand or even hugging me, welcoming me to the party, and telling me how grateful they were for my work. At first I could attach names to faces — Montse, Justin Lambert, Asha. But soon the beer, the pot-infused air, the strange orange lighting and the deafening noise began to take their toll. After a while, I couldn't remember anyone's name, even my own.

I introduced Tiffany to people as best I could. But in truth, she was reduced to the role of admiring and supportive partner — smiling proudly while attention focused on me. She performed her role loyally.

Why were people thanking me for my work? In terms of stopping the pile driver, I'd been a total failure. In fact, the Midnight TRO seemed a monument to the proposition that pursuing legal remedies was a waste of time and self-help the only way to go. But if the residents of Waldo Point wanted to overlook my checkered past and treat me like an honored guest, why should I complain?

By the time people stopped coming up to me, my ears had adjusted — somewhat — to the decibel level. I proposed to Tiffany that we go listen to the band. She agreed, and after a quick return to the bar we squeezed our way to a standing space just in front of the group.

They were four dudes and a lone chick. The men were all shaggy to the nth degree, dressed in combinations of black and orange, or at least so the lighting made it seem. The woman — tall, stick-thin and bespectacled — had blond hair down to her waist.

The band played classic rock, heavy on the blues, music that took you back to the heyday of the Rolling Stones and Eric Clapton. Apparently they wrote all their own songs; at least, I didn't recognize any covers.

The name of the group, I learned, was the Redlegs. They were all Waldo Point residents, though they played throughout the Bay Area. My informant gave me the names of all the members, but only one stuck in my mind. The tall, thin woman's name was Maggie Catfish.

Were the Redlegs really that good? Or was it the beer in my system, the contact high, the exotic lighting, the energy of the crowd? In any event, for number after number, I stood mesmerized.

Eventually I turned and realized Tiffany was no longer standing beside me. She had disappeared.

I set out to find her, stopping first, however, for another beer. Unfortunately, with the Midnight TRO's warehouse-like interior packed with hundreds of people, finding Tiffany posed a baffling challenge. I shouldered my way through the crowd in one direction, then another, not sure what I was doing.

At some point I noticed that at the back of the barge two small rooms opened off the main room. I looked into the first room and saw no one I knew. Then I looked into the second and saw Tiffany and Becky, sitting next to each other on the edge of a bed, engaged in an intimate conversation, and sharing a joint. Becky in her outrageous leopard-print costume; Tiffany more demure and covered-up in a long-sleeved lavender dress. Not that Tiffany was unsexy; her sleeves were sheer, unlined voile.

I hesitated. What was going on? Were they talking about me?

And why was Tiffany smoking pot? I knew she had in college, but I thought that after moving back to San Francisco, she'd given it up.

A few seconds later, I realized I was being ridiculous. What did I have to fear? I'd never acted in any way improperly or suggestively toward Becky. Maybe in fantasy, but not in reality.

Instead of panicking, I should take advantage of the situation. In the past, I had compared Tiffany's and Becky's distinctive types of beauty — Tiffany's silken smoothness as opposed to Becky's surfer-girl freshness. Now that I could observe the two of them sitting side by side, I should pursue the comparison further.

The problem was that in the peculiar interior lighting of the Midnight TRO, they both looked simply orange.

I decided to make myself known. Walking up to the pair, I asked, "What are you two talking about?"

Tiffany looked up, eyes unfocused. "Chocolate mousse."

"Chocolate mousse? Really? I didn't know you were interested in chocolate mousse."

She seemed flustered. "You're right. I'm not. . . . Normally. . . . But Becky here has this *amazing* recipe for chocolate mousse, so while I may not be interested in chocolate mousse in general, I am interested in Becky's very special chocolate mousse." She offered a toothy smile.

Enough of chocolate mousse. Changing the subject, I said, "I didn't know you still smoked dope"

"Oh well, some nights Kimberley and I have something to smoke."

Kimberley was one of her San Francisco roommates. So this is what Tiff did on the nights we weren't together.

Becky stood up, saying, "I'd better be getting back to the party. I'm supposed to be helping manage the thing. As if anything at Waldo Point can be managed."

Tiffany and Becky gave each other a long, affectionate hug. As Becky departed, Tiffany turned to me and said, "Want to go listen to the band some more?"

We listened, we drank. We exchanged pleasantries with strangers. It was too crowded to dance, but we swayed back and forth to the Redleg's infectious melodies.

I was proud of the way Tiffany fit in and enjoyed herself. The environment could hardly have differed more from her usual haunts; she knew no one in the crowd other than me; yet she thrived. If it was a test, she passed.

Walking back to our car at the end of the evening, a crescent moon shining down on us, I drew her close to my side and asked, "So, did that qualify as midnight dances with unspeakable rites?"

She snuggled even tighter. "Close enough."

17
MEETING WITH SAM

I knew the meeting was going to be heavy when Sam closed the door to his office. He was usually an open-door kind of guy. And given the photo that had appeared front-page center in the weekend edition of the *Independent-Journal*— of the sunken barge at Waldo Point, emblazoned with the name "MIDNIGHT TRO" — I had a fairly good idea what the heaviness was going to be about.

Sam looked grim. "I just talked to Larry Klein — "

Klein was the president of Marin Legal Aid's board of directors.

" — and he in turn had just talked to Judge Daley. The judge saw the photo in the Sunday *I-J* and, as you might guess, is mightily pissed."

I looked down and said nothing.

"Not only that, without consulting with me first, Larry apologized to the judge and promised him that in the future, Marin Legal Aid wouldn't represent — and here I quote Larry directly — 'anyone found to have been part of the sinking of the Midnight TRO barge.'"

A coppery taste seeped into my mouth. "'Anyone found to have part of the sinking of the Midnight TRO barge,'" I repeated. "What does the word 'found' in that phrase mean? Convicted in a court of law?"

Sam grimaced. "That's the thing about Larry. You can never tell whether he's being really clever or he's simply confused. In any event, I didn't ask him to clarify. I thought if it was left vague, we'd have more wiggle room."

I held my head in my hands. "Thanks for salvaging . . . what you could."

Sam gave me fifteen seconds of silence to absorb this bad news. Then he continued, "I've always said that if we're not making some people mad, we're not doing our job. So in that sense, representing these houseboat people is exactly the sort of thing we ought to be doing.

"On the other hand, we don't want to be making so many people mad that we're all fired, and Marin Legal Aid goes out of business. It's a balancing act."

Sam looked at me as if expecting a response. I managed to squeeze out, "Right."

After a few more seconds of silence, Sam said, "There's another part to this I need to bring up. For the past couple of months, Judith has been bending my ear about your spending most of your time on the houseboaters. She says you're hogging all the time available for impact work, and she's stuck doing all the service work."

Judith's resentment didn't come as a surprise. The reigning theory in legal services for the poor was that every legal aid office should strike a balance between "service cases" — routine welfare hearings, employment issues, social security problems, evictions and so forth — and "impact litigation" — cases that had the potential to benefit more than just a single client. Impact work was generally the more interesting and rewarding of the two, and hence each attorney wanted her or his share. It was basically true that for two months I'd been hogging all the time Marin Legal Aid had available for impact work.

"You know the Canal group she's been working with?" Sam asked.

"Yeah." The Canal District in east San Rafael was heavily Hispanic and one of the few areas of concentrated poverty in Marin County.

"They're planning a rent strike, and Judith wants to bring a big habitability suit in conjunction. But right now, she's so swamped with service work she doesn't have the time."

I took a deep breath. "I understand."

"I may as well tell you exactly what she said, just so you know. As soon as she heard about the Midnight TRO, she came to me and said, 'Why is Marin Legal Aid representing these thugs down at Waldo Point when we don't have time to represent all the single mothers and people of color in the Canal District? Those houseboat people *choose* to live in squalor. The people in the Canal District don't have any other choice.'"

Thugs? Ouch. I was too shaken to say anything.

"Now I don't consider the houseboaters thugs," Sam tried to reassure me. "Or at least not all of them. But we do need to clear up some time for Judith to put together her habitability suit."

"Right. I'll shift back to service work for a while."

Sam nodded, picked up a pen, and twirled it with his index and middle fingers.

"Exactly what did we promise the houseboaters we'd do?" he asked. "We promised them we'd file a lawsuit to stop the project, which we've done. We promised them we'd go in for a TRO, which we've done, for better or for worse. Was there anything else?"

"We said if anyone at Waldo Point got served with an unlawful detainer, they should come in, and if they're eligible, we'd represent them."

"Right, right. But at least for the time being, there aren't any Waldo Point UDs coming in, correct?"

"Correct."

"Anything else?"

"I've urged them to think about negotiations. So far they haven't shown any interest, but if they do, I'd like to be available to provide advice. If they ask."

Sam twirled his pen some more. Finally he said, "I don't think that should be a problem, as long as it doesn't take up too much time. Anything else?"

I thought for a moment. "No."

"Good. See you at the attorneys' meeting tomorrow. You'll be picking up a bunch of new service cases."

I tried to smile. "Can't wait."

18
BECKY COMES UP WITH A PLAN

Fortunately, I never had to say "no" to the Waldo Point houseboat community. For two months following the sinking of the Midnight TRO, all was quiet on the Richardson Bay waterfront. Strawberry Point Harbor Associates made no effort to free or reactivate the pile driver. The county sent no sheriff's deputies to Waldo Point. No unlawful detainers were served.

As the silence from Waldo Point lengthened, I began to worry that things were in fact happening there, but for whatever reason, the community had switched its legal business to another attorney.

In this vein, I remembered that at the time of their greatest crisis — the arrival of the pile driver — the houseboaters had called, before calling me, an attorney named Ray Alencar. I decided to do some checking on Ray Alencar.

Turned out he was a big-time criminal-defense attorney, specializing in drug cases. He had the reputation of being the lawyer to go to if you were charged with a drug-related offense, and was said to have as clients all the top drug dealers and marijuana growers in several counties.

My discovery that the houseboaters, or at least some of them, hung out with a major pillar of the drug world troubled me. But by now I'd grown accustomed to turning a blind eye to the houseboaters' deviations from the straight and narrow.

More to the point, I worried that if Ray Alencar was in fact a rival of mine for the position of number-one attorney to the houseboaters, he would be formidable competition.

He was older, more experienced, more famous, and probably a better attorney.

I eventually called Kevin, seeking reassurance. He relieved me of my worries. Things were as calm as they seemed, he said, and if anything happened, I'd be the first to know.

Meanwhile, throwing myself back into service work, I immediately noticed a steep rise in evictions. Home prices had exploded earlier; now rents were following suit. No rent control laws existed anywhere in Marin County, and as a result landlords could raise rents as much as they wanted. Our clients couldn't pay the new, higher rents, but they didn't move out either, because they had nowhere else to go. Sooner or later a process server bearing an unlawful detainer would find them, and at that point they came to us.

There was little we could do for these people, other than try to negotiate with the landlord's attorney for more time for the client to move out. Sometimes we were successful, sometimes not. In any event, the onslaught of eviction cases from all over the county made clear that the plight of the Waldo Point houseboat community was but one facet of a broader phenomenon: In the competition for living space in Marin County, the rich were muscling out the poor.

Then one day I received a call from Becky. She had something to show me. A plan, one that might someday become a basis for negotiations. Did I have time to come to Waldo Point for a brief meeting?

Becky's smoky, sexy voice brought back happy memories. "Yes, of course."

The meeting took place on the boat Becky and Kevin shared. Kevin met me in the parking lot and guided me there, but this time I made a conscious effort to remember the route, so that in the future I wouldn't need a guide.

The boat consisted of a blue-painted, L-shaped structure perched on a barge, with an ample deck inside the L. Plants and tchotchkes — a pair of moose antlers, a set of Soleri windbells, a small concrete Cupid — filled the deck. At one edge a tall pole bore cutout wooden circles on which were painted colorful geometric shapes — an orange triangle, a blue circle.

The interior of the boat continued the theme of oddities and knickknacks. Scattered here and there were a lava lamp, a mosaic peace sign, a piece of driftwood, an abalone shell, an antique-looking telescope, an ashtray resembling a cabbage leaf and a chunk of purple amethyst. A dream catcher, a Winterland poster advertising a Jefferson Airplane concert, and a macramé hanging adorned the walls, along with photos of the three of the four Beatles (Paul mysteriously missing), a clock with a ladybug face, and a set of photos of what looked like a family vacation in the north woods.

A kitchen blended into a dining area, which in turn blended into a living area. A side door led to what was presumably the bedroom. The smell of burnt wood led my eyes to the wood stove in the kitchen. A faint trace of scented candle suggested flames of a more romantic nature.

Four people were waiting for me when I arrived: Becky, Kevin, their neighbor Montse and another woman named Karen. Notably, neither Achille nor Hank was present. Becky wore a blue-and-white baseball jersey with a rainbow-colored logo reading "Camp Wish-a-Rainbow," and below that pink shorts that left large expanses of bare leg exposed.

The four stood around a table on which rested a blueprint-sized sheet of paper. That sheet was the purpose of the meeting. Drawn up by Becky, it was a plan for an alternative redevelopment of Waldo Point.

To start, Becky showed me a small copy of the plan the county approved in 1974. That plan was simplicity itself: five long, straight piers sticking out insolently into Richardson Bay.

Then she showed me her plan. What she'd done was take the 1974 plan, put more thought into it, modify it, refine it, massage it, and end up with a plan that created a "small-boat harbor" in which 110 SOW boats could be accommodated.

How had she accomplished this? First, under the 1974 plan Strawberry Point Harbor Associates had the right to create 285 large berths, all of which they could rent out for whatever the market would bear. Becky had reduced this number of "market-rate" berths from 285 to 245, a cut of 40 berths.

Second, the 110 berths in the new small-boat harbor were much smaller than the market-rate berths.

Finally, and most importantly, she'd reworked the original plan — breaking up straight lines into more flexible arrangements, adjusting lines to natural contours, and utilizing areas wasted before. As a result, even though she was increasing overall density by 70 berths — 110 berths added in the small-boat harbor minus 40 market-rate berths eliminated — her plan looked more open, more relaxed, with more privacy and better views, than the original plan.

I studied her 36" x 48" plan several minutes, admiring its detail. Becky had outlined every single berth, 355 in all.

"Wow!" I said, straightening up. "This is amazing. I'd never realized how stupid and unimaginative the plan approved by the county really is. Five straight piers jutting out into the bay. I just thought that's the way all houseboat marinas are designed. How should I know? I'd never seen a plan for a houseboat marina before. But now that I see your plan, I realize there's so much more that can be done."

Becky caught my eye and smiled proudly. "Do you know the history of the county's plan?" she asked. "For years Don Arques had been fending off the county's efforts to get him to do something about Waldo Point. But finally they told him, 'You have to submit a plan.' So Arques told his assistant, D. B. Luther — you remember him, the guy who testified, or really *didn't* testify, at the Owl trial — Arques told D. B., 'You go draw up a plan.' So D. B. went into his office, took out a pen and a ruler, found a map of the property, and drew five straight lines on it. The whole process took him about half an hour. That's the plan that was submitted to the county, and that's the plan the county approved."

"That's sad." I said. "Your plan is so much better. But we've got to be realistic. Strawberry Point Harbor Associates are going to go bananas if and when they see this."

"Actually, they shouldn't. They're losing 40 market-rate berths, but they're gaining 110 new berths in the small-boat harbor. If the residents of the small-boat harbor pay on average 36 percent of what the market-rate tenants pay, Strawberry Point Harbor Associates will come out even. So what difference should it make to them?"

I paused for a moment to go through the calculations in my head.

"You'd have some sort of rent-control system in the small-boat harbor?"

"Correct. We'd probably have to work with the county on that."

My admiration of Becky, both her beauty and her intellect, scaled new heights. Standing next to her, imbibing her rosy scent, engaging in a serious one-on-one conversation on significant topics, her attention focused on me as if the other people in the room didn't exist, an intensity both intellectual and physical flowing between us, I felt life could not be sweeter.

"But what about the SOW membership?" I asked. "In that census you took, how many boats were there at Waldo Point?"

"One hundred eighty-five. And there are only 110 berths in the small-boat harbor on this plan. So obviously there's a discrepancy. But for several reasons we think 110 is in fact about the right number.

"First place, we took another poll, and about 35 percent of the people who responded said they didn't want to be part of any situation where they had to pay rent. Now maybe some of these people would change their minds if they were actually confronted with the choice of either paying rent or being kicked out. But it definitely shows that the idea of being part of a normal, legalized, rent-paying, law-aiding houseboat marina is not an idea that appeals to everyone here. So why shouldn't those who *aren't* interested just step aside and let those who *are* interested do their thing?

"Another question is, how many people here can afford even a minimal berthage. In this same poll we asked another question: "Could you afford to pay $50 per month in berthage?" Only 53 percent said they could; 47 percent said they couldn't.

"Now we can look for government programs and subsidies to help out. And maybe some of the people who voted no in this poll were just trying to establish a bargaining position, so to speak. But still, it shows that even at 110 berths and a very low rent, we might struggle to find enough boats to fill all the berths.

"And I'm not willing to fight for the idea we should all be able to live here for free. There are people down here who feel that way, and of course they're entitled to their opinions. But I don't feel that way. I don't think it's reasonable to say we should all be able to live here for free in perpetuity, and I think if we say that, we're bound to lose."

By now I was wondering which of us was the attorney; Becky's arguments were crafted like a legal brief. I also wondered if she might be protesting too much. The fact she had all these finely-honed, statistics-laden arguments to show that 110 was an adequate number might indicate she was worried about how the SOW membership would greet her proposal.

"How are you going to proceed with his plan procedurally?" I asked. "Will you present it to the SOW membership and let them discuss it? Do they get to vote on it? Or is this your own personal plan, not a SOW plan?"

"We'll present it to the SOW membership, and they'll discuss and vote on it. If they approve, we'll go ahead and try to sell it to the Strawberries and the county. And if the SOW membership doesn't approve it, then" — she shrugged, a glum look on her face — "it's dead."

For more than an hour the five of us — Kevin, Montse and Karen joined in at this point — discussed issues arising from Becky's plan. Who would build the small-boat harbor? Who would maintain it? Who would collect the rents? How would the rents be regulated? Could the members of SOW form some sort of co-op that might undertake some or all of these tasks? Would the best idea be for SOW to enter into a master lease with Strawberry Point Harbor Associates and then sublet the individual berths in the small-boat harbor to its members? Eventually, we realized our minds were so filled with new and confusing ideas we had to stop.

"Okay," I said. "All this looks very promising. And if you need help in trying to implement this plan, I'd be happy to work with you. Delighted, in fact. But it seems like first you have to sell it to your members."

"Right," said Becky, her voice low and sultry. "And that's our job."

19
CUP OF COFFEE

As I was getting up to leave, Kevin said, "Rick, this is the first time you've visited our pad. Do you have a few minutes? Why don't you stay and have a cup of coffee with us?"

I hadn't any more than the usual number of emergencies that day, so I said yes. Becky rolled up her plan, put a rubber band around it, and leaned it against the wall, thereby turning the worktable back to a dining table. Then she headed to a Mr. Coffee machine.

Once hot cups of coffee were in our hands, I said, "I don't really know anything about the two of you, except for your roles in SOW. Tell me something about yourselves. Where are you from, and how did you happen to end up in Waldo Point?"

Becky and Kevin looked at each other. She signaled to him to go first.

"Where am I from? Morristown, New Jersey. How did I happen to end up here? I dropped out of journalism school at Rutgers, based on the idea — the totally impractical idea, I might add — of supporting myself by traveling around the country writing and selling freelance articles. I'd made my way to San Francisco on the theory that was where a lot of exciting stuff was happening, and I should be able to find some interesting topics for articles. Then about a month after I arrived, I met a guy in a bar who told me that up in Marin County there was this community of, quote, vegetarian hippie pirates, unquote. I figured vegetarian hippie pirates would make a cool story, so I headed up here. And once I got here, I never left."

"How did you get out of the draft?"

"Three twenty-two."

Lucky stiff. He had a high number. I had to spend months going to doctors and building up a pile of medical reports to get out.

I turned to Becky. "What about you?"

She seemed reluctant to answer. Finally she said, "I'm from Wisconsin."

"Where in Wisconsin?"

"A little place in the country you've never heard of."

I waited for more, but Becky remained silent. She picked up the piece of amethyst and began fingering it. I wondered if I'd unwittingly crossed a red line.

Then Becky said, "I guess I should tell you, even though it's a little embarrassing. My parents are the leaders of a fundamentalist Christian cult, and I grew up in a religious commune. I came to San Francisco because that was as far away from the New Jerusalem of the North — that's what my parents call their place — as I could get with the money I had at the time. I lived for two years in the Haight-Ashbury, and while I was there I met some people from Waldo Point. I came up here one weekend and, just like Kevin, fell in love with the place. I've been here ever since."

I was so taken aback by Becky's answer that at first I couldn't think of a response. At last I asked, "Are you still in touch with your parents?"

Again Becky took a lengthy pause before answering, still fingering the piece of amethyst. "It depends on what you mean by 'in touch.' We talk on the phone every once in a while, but the conversation consists mostly of them telling me I'm going to hell and should come back immediately. I never have a chance to get a word in edgewise."

"Have they ever been here to Waldo Point?"

"Lord no. As a matter of fact, they don't even know I live here. All they know is that I have a post-office box in Sausalito."

I found it hard to fathom Becky's upbringing, so different from my own secular and urban start in life. On the other hand, it was easy to see why, after childhood spent in a repressive religious commune, she found anarchic, rule-free Waldo Point so appealing.

I turned back to Kevin. "What about you? Are you in touch with your parents?"

"With my mom, definitely. She's actually quite decent. She's a politician — a member of the New Jersey General Assembly."

"Really? Democrat or Republican?"

"Democrat."

"Has she ever visited you here at Waldo Point?"

"Oh yes."

"How did she take it? Was she shocked?"

Kevin smiled and shook his head. "I don't think I could shock my mom. She's pretty unshockable."

"But what did she say? Did she make any comments?"

"Not really. She just took it all in, asked a few questions, and smiled."

"What about your father?"

"My actual father is three husbands ago in terms of my mom. He didn't last long, and he's never played a major role in my life, either here or back in New Jersey."

"I do have a stepfather, though." Kevin chuckled. "Tell you a funny story about him. He came here with my mom that time. All the time they were touring around, looking at boats, he didn't say a word. Then we came back here to our boat and had some drinks; he still didn't say a word. I was beginning to wonder if he was mute or had some sort of speech impediment. Then, just as they were about to leave, he turned to me and said, 'Have you ever thought about joining the army?'"

Kevin, Becky and I all broke out laughing.

"What about you?" Kevin asked, looking at me. "We've told you about ourselves. Tell us something about yourself."

I looked down and sighed. "My life seems so dull compared to yours. It's all been lockstep. I went to high school in Pasadena, where I grew up. Then directly to UCLA for college. Then directly to Berkeley for law school. Then directly to Marin Legal Aid. No big adventures along the way, not even any time outs. Of course, part of it was I was trying to avoid the draft. But even if the draft hadn't existed, I probably would have done the same thing."

"Your life can't be all that dull if you're representing us," Becky said.

I laughed. "I guess not."

"Becky raises a good question, though," said Kevin. "How did you end up representing a bunch of houseboaters?"

I shrugged. "Because I was on intake duty the day you two plus Hank chose to walk into Legal Aid."

Struck by the role chance sometimes plays in our lives, everyone remained silent for a moment.

"But there's another question behind that," Kevin insisted. "How did you happen to be working at Marin Legal Aid?"

"That's a good question. Well, when I was in law school, I worked the first summer for a big commercial law firm in downtown LA. Then the second summer I worked for San Francisco Neighborhood Legal Assistance, which is the San Francisco equivalent to our Marin Legal Aid. I enjoyed the work at Neighborhood Legal Assistance much more than the work at the big commercial firm. So when it came time to look for a job, I focused on legal services organizations."

"Why do you think that was the case — that you enjoyed the legal aid office more than the big commercial firm?" asked Kevin. He definitely had a journalist's instincts, an urge to dig deep.

I didn't have an immediate answer. Finally I said, "It's probably relevant that my father's a lawyer, and he works for a big commercial firm in downtown LA. He's very successful, in fact. He has clients like ARCO and Security Pacific Bank.

"I always wanted to be a lawyer, but I didn't want to just follow in my father's footsteps. I needed to be my own man. And going into legal services, which is sort of a one-hundred-eighty-degree turn from what he does, seemed to meet that need. Does that make sense?"

"Sure. Was the commercial firm in downtown LA you worked for while you were in law school your father's firm?"

"No. But it was in the same building. Ten floors below, to be exact. So you'd have to say my father was hovering above me. Literally."

Kevin and Becky smiled knowingly.

"If you really want to step off the straight and narrow path," said Kevin, "why don't you move here to Waldo Point? Nobody would mistake you for your father then."

I smiled. "Thanks, but no thanks."

"Why not? We'll find you a boat. You don't have to build one."

The grins on Kevin and Becky's faces reassured me they were jesting. I therefore didn't need to answer truthfully — that much as I valued the houseboat community as a client,

I had no desire whatsoever to live in a place as muddy, visually chaotic, crowded and unsafe as Waldo Point.

But what to say instead?

At last I came up with, "An apple, or at least this apple, can fall only so far from the tree."

"Fair enough," said Kevin, smiling.

"While we're all in a gossipy mood," I said, "tell me about Achille. Where did he come from?"

Kevin and Becky looked at each other, as if each hoping the other would answer. Finally Becky said, "You've probably heard the business about his being a member of the Byzantine royal family."

"Yes, Hank told me."

She rolled her eyes. "Personally, I find that a little ridiculous."

"Do you know what he did before he came to Waldo Point?"

"Basically, he lived off the ladies. He lived in a number of places around North Beach — this is in San Francisco in the 1950s, the beatnik period. He had these women friends, and he would stay with one or another of them for a few months, or even a year at a time. The women would buy all the food and generally take care of expenses. This type of arrangement, with the women supporting their philosopher boyfriends or poet boyfriends, was fairly common during the beatnik period."

"Did Achille work during this period?"

"He might have worked a few hours a week at a bookstore or something like that. But never any real job."

In other words Achille the Byzantine Satyr was also Achille the Leach.

"How did he happen to come to Waldo Point?" I asked.

"Through some friends he heard that the cabin on top of the *San Rafael* was up for grabs. He came over, talked to

Donlon Arques, and they came to some sort of deal. I'm not sure of the details, but I know Achille has Arques' permission to be where he is."

"But even assuming he gets free rent, how does he support himself otherwise, like for food and pipe tobacco?"

"I think he gets SSI."

"Do you know where he's from originally?"

"New York."

A thought came to me. "Waldo Point is like an archeology dig. It has layers of history on top of each other. Hank is left over from the Marinship shipbuilding enterprise of the 1940s. Achille is a refugee from the beatnik movement and the North Beach of the 50s. And you and a lot of other people here are refuges from the hippie movement and the Haight-Ashbury of the 1960s."

"You're absolutely right," said Kevin.

"So don't bitch at us when we're not as together as you'd like us to be," Becky said, laughing.

I left Becky and Kevin's boat soon after that, in a buoyant mood. For the first time I could see a path to a successful resolution of the crisis at Waldo Point. The houseboaters seemed to have developed a leadership core that was reasonable and willing to meet the county halfway. And Becky's plan provided an ingenious and workable solution to the problem of competing interests claiming the same space. Hopefully all the time and emotional energy I had spent on the houseboaters' cause would someday be vindicated.

Of the troubles that lay in store, I had no inkling.

20
DINNER AT THE WONGS

Around the same time Tiffany and I crossed a major threshold. We decided to move in together.

It was not an easy decision. Much as Tiff and I both wanted to take this next step, a serious obstacle existed — our respective workplaces. I worked in San Rafael, she in downtown San Francisco. While the two locales were only about twenty miles apart, those twenty miles included a major bottleneck — the Golden Gate Bridge. Not only did crossing the bridge cost a dollar a day, there was always the possibility of an accident, a backup, a delay. Even without an accident, getting across the bridge on a Friday afternoon in summer was a guaranteed nightmare. I didn't want to commute across the bridge from San Francisco. Tiff didn't want to commute to the city from Marin.

We'd finally agreed on a way to resolve the impasse. We would look for an apartment together, and we would look in both the southern tip of Marin — basically Sausalito and Mill Valley — and the northern tip of San Francisco — the Richmond and Marina districts. Once we'd seen a decent number of possibilities, we would rank them based on rent level, square footage, condition, light, parking, and so forth — all the considerations that go into choosing an apartment except for location. In other words, the process would be location neutral, no preference for either Marin or San Francisco. We would end up with the best available apartment for the money in either southern Marin or northern San Francisco, and wherever that apartment was located would be the side of the bridge on which we would live.

There was also one more obstacle to our living together. I'd never met Tiffany's parents. They knew of my existence and knew something about me — including the crucial fact I was white — but we'd never met face-to-face. And Tiffany wouldn't feel comfortable living a few miles from her parents' residence with a man they'd never met.

Complicating the situation, Tiffany seemed leery about introducing the three of us, and I wasn't exactly sure why. From time to time she mentioned her parents were hoping she would "meet a nice Chinese boy, get married and settle down." She also said her mother didn't speak much English. I wondered if she might be hesitant to show off a mother and father who worked as a maid and maintenance man respectively at the downtown Hilton hotel.

In any event, now that we were planning to move in together, procrastination had to end. We would all have dinner together. Nothing would be said at the dinner about our living-together plans, but the way would be paved for her to break the news to her parents sometime later.

The Wongs lived in the Sunset district of San Francisco, out by the ocean's edge, an area known for its fog. When Tiffany and I arrived at their house promptly at six, the moist air had transformed the street on which they lived into a vague Impressionist painting. Getting out of the car, that same air smelled of seagulls and Chinese cooking. From what I could tell through the mist, all the houses on the street looked exactly the same — two narrow stories, garage below, living quarters above, stairway off to one side.

Mr. and Mrs. Wong greeted us warmly at the door. Cooking smells — chicken broth, soy sauce and a myriad I couldn't identify — filled the air.

Mr. Wong, short and bald, wore a tan sports coat, patterned tie, white dress shirt and gray trousers. He was dressed more formally than I was. I had on only a sweater and shirt to go with my khakis.

Tiffany had told me her mother was considerably younger than her father, and it showed in her pleasing face and gleaming black hair. The rest of her, however, was enveloped in a floral kitchen apron wrapped around a pale green pantsuit.

Also present was Tiffany's younger brother, Wilson, a thin, mop-haired, bespectacled lad who looked younger than his twenty-three years.

We headed to the living room, small and filled with furniture that looked too big for the space. Following Tiffany's advice, I had brought a bottle of wine, an expensive Jordan chardonnay. The Wongs seemed delighted. I opened the bottle, and the five of us exchanged toasts.

After only a couple of sips of wine, Mrs. Wong disappeared, and the rest of us headed to the dining room, where the table was covered with a plastic tablecloth and set with Chinese porcelain plates and bowls and both chopsticks and forks. Since we were now nearer the kitchen, the air bore an even stronger fragrance of Mrs. Wong's exotic cooking smells.

Mrs. Wong began bringing out individual bowls of soup. The soup was clear, with what looked liked chunks of pear in it. Mrs. Wong said to me something that sounded like "meron."

"It's winter melon soup," Tiffany said.

The soup was delicious, the crunchy vegetable infused with a rich chicken broth. I'd never tasted anything like it before.

As we were slurping our soup, Mr. Wong looked at Tiffany and me and asked, "Where two of you meet?"

I looked at Tiffany. "Mutual friends," she answered. "We were introduced by mutual friends."

This was a complete lie. We'd met in a bar and introduced ourselves to each other. But in preparing for the night's dinner, Tiff and I had agreed that "mutual friends" would sell better than "met in a bar."

No sooner had I spooned out the last of my soup than Mrs. Wong's hand was whisking my bowl away and she was saying, "I get you more." I acquiesced, and soon I was enjoying a second bowl of winter melon soup.

"You from Southern California?" Mr. Wong asked me.

"Yes. Pasadena."

"Where you go to school?"

"I went to UCLA for undergraduate and Boalt, Berkeley, for law school."

"Good schools," said Mr. Wong, obviously pleased.

Once the soup was finished and our bowls cleared, Mrs. Wong began bringing out large platters and bowls heaped with hot, steaming food. Tofu with black bean sauce and pork bits. Soy-sauce chicken. Mixed vegetables. Finally, on a charger plate, a whole steamed fish.

"This is fabulous," I said.

And indeed it was. Tiffany had mentioned her mother was a good cook, but I wasn't expecting a feast like this. In the tofu dish, the pungent black bean sauce contrasted exquisitely with the soft, silky tofu. The velvety soy-sauce chicken tasted almost sweet, with a hint of licorice. The mixed vegetables — snow peas, carrots, napa cabbage, celery and onions — burst with freshness. And the whole fish, infused with ginger and scallions, was flaky, succulent and much easier to eat than I'd feared.

After a period of silent eating, Mr. Wong looked at me and said, "Tiffany say you work for people who live on houseboats."

"Yes. That's right."

"I see them on TV. They look like hippies."

"True. A lot of them do look like hippies"

"These people, they work?"

"Some do. Some don't. Or they work on their boats, or trade work with other people in the community."

"How much they pay you?"

"Actually, they don't pay me anything. I work for a nonprofit agency, called Marin Legal Aid, and I get paid by it. Legal Aid represents only people who qualify as low-income, and we don't charge for our services."

"You mean houseboat people get law work for free?"

I didn't like where this was going, but couldn't see an escape hatch. "Yes. As I said, Legal Aid is set up to provide free legal services to people who qualify as low-income. And a survey was done that showed a large majority of the people in the houseboat community are low-income."

Mr. Wong's look turned sour. "If I go to lawyer, I have to pay."

"That's probably true."

He shook his head in disgust. "They don't work, so they get lawyer for free. I work hard, but if I need lawyer, I pay a lot." He kept shaking his head and pursing his lips.

Fortunately, floppy-haired Wilson entered the conversation at this point. "I hear there's a lot of drug-dealing over there where the houseboats are. So I was wondering, like, if that's really true."

"Um, I try not to notice or ask questions about things like that."

Wilson looked disappointed.

Every time I finished one of the helpings on my plate, Mrs. Wong would immediately pop up, pick up the relevant serving bowl or platter, hover it over my plate, serving spoon in hand, and ask, "You want more?" Striving to please, I kept saying yes, but I was feeling increasingly full.

"Your job with this agency, job good?" Mr. Wong asked.

"It's okay. I'm happy with it at the current moment."

"Pay good?"

"Unfortunately, that's the bad part. Pay's enough to get by on, but I'd be making more money if I were with a private firm."

"You can't get job with private firm?"

"I probably could if I made an effort at it. But I'm happy where I am now. At least for the time being. I can always go over to the private side later."

"So right now, you not make as much money as you could?"

"Yes, I guess you could say that."

"I think you make mistake. Time to make money is when young. Then don't have to worry about money when old." Mr. Wong nodded in agreement with his own aphorism.

Oh shit, I've blown it again.

Once again clueless brother Wilson came to my rescue. Breaking the silence that followed Mr. Wong's remark, he said, "I know you said you don't ask a lot of questions around the houseboats. But I was wondering, like, if you knew, just from your general knowledge and that sort of thing — because you're from Marin, right? — if you knew whether pot prices in Marin, considering the fact it's nearer to the sources — you know, Mendocino, Humboldt — whether pot prices in Marin are, like, lower than they are here in San Francisco, where they're really, really high?"

As Mr. Wong glared at him, Wilson looked agonized by San Francisco's high pot prices.

"I can't answer that," I said, confident I'd regained moral high ground.

Mrs. Wong kept urging seconds, thirds, even fourths on me, but by this time I was ready to explode. Despite the risk of offending, I started to say no. Though I did have a couple of almond cookies for dessert.

When Tiffany and I left, the fog outside had thickened to the point we could barely see twenty feet ahead. Tiffany squeezed me to her side.

"That went well," she said.

"You thought so? I thought just the opposite. Seemed like every time I opened my mouth, I ended up in an argument with your father."

"Oh, don't worry about it." She squeezed me even tighter. "You ate Mom's cooking, and that's what matters." She turned to me, her eyes wide with wonder. "You ate a lot of it, as a matter of fact. I was amazed."

21
MEMBERSHIP MEETING

I received a call from Kevin. SOW was holding a membership meeting to discuss Becky's plan for a 110-berth small-boat harbor. SOW wanted me to be there in the role of legal advisor.

"Why do I need to be there? Isn't the main issue that Becky's plan raises the question whether SOW should settle for a number of berths that's less than the number of boats there now. And if that's the issue, it seems to me it's one you need to settle among yourselves. It's an economic issue, or maybe a moral issue. Certainly not a legal issue. I don't see why I should have any say."

"I hear what you're saying, but the board would very much like for you to be there. There's a danger of the meeting going seriously off-track, with a lot of mistaken ideas about our legal situation. And if you're there, we can keep things under control."

"What about Dan Porter?" He was the attorney I'd worked with on the TRO who lived at Waldo Point.

"He's not impartial. He wants to talk at the meeting as a member, not a lawyer."

I didn't relish serving as the board's designated defender against the crazier elements of the SOW membership. But in the end, I agreed to come.

The meeting took place in the evening. When I arrived at 7:30, the sun was just setting.

SOW had put together a meeting space in one corner of the parking lot. Someone had constructed a small wooden platform, and on that platform sat two folding chairs.

Facing the platform were at least a hundred and fifty people, splayed out in a fan shape and making do with a variety of seating arrangements. Three aged wooden benches provided seating for some. Other SOW members sat on the ground, on blankets, on cushions, on folding chairs, on crates, on barrels. Achille sat up front in a ratty wingback armchair, his young girlfriend by his side.

To one side was a large bonfire, several men tending it. The April evening was cloudy and starless, the lights of Bridgeway far away, and hence as twilight vanished in the course of the meeting, the bonfire provided almost the only light. It made everyone look one-sided — left side lit, right side invisible.

The air smelled of saltwater, sewage, wood smoke and cigarette smoke. It also seemed full of tension. I thought back to the morning after the sinking of the Midnight TRO and the party the subsequent Saturday night. Then the members of SOW had been boisterous, exuberant, high-spirited. Tonight everyone seemed grim, anxious, reluctant to talk.

One of the two chairs on the platform was, I learned, for me. Once again, I was being cast in a larger role than I wanted.

The other chair was for the person who would moderate the meeting, a man in his early thirties with the usual waterfront young male look — blond, beefy, tanned — except this particular exemplar was a size larger than usual. I was introduced to him, but immediately forgot his name.

He was, to my surprise, not a SOW member, nor even a resident of Waldo Point. Instead, he was from Napa Street Pier, a small houseboat community located further south along the waterfront, inside Sausalito. Apparently all the officers of SOW — Achille, Kevin, Becky and so forth — had declined to serve as moderator on the ground they wanted to participate in the debate. To find a moderator who didn't have strong feelings he or she wanted to express, SOW had had to turn to an outsider.

The moderator and I stepped onto the platform, and I sat down. I felt unpleasantly exposed. At least there was no spotlight, only the twilight and flickering flames of the fire. The moderator called the meeting to order in a loud, authoritative voice. I could see why he was chosen. Once the crowd settled down, he turned the meeting over to Becky.

She didn't need to explain the physical layout of her proposed small-boat harbor; the plan had been posted for all to see for several days. Instead she spent most of her time explaining how the harbor would be managed and the rents controlled. The thinking here had evolved considerably since the meeting I'd attended on her boat.

The concept now was that the members of SOW would form a cooperative, and this cooperative would enter into a long-term master lease for the small-boat harbor from Strawberry Point Harbor Associates, the property owner. The co-op would then manage the harbor and collect the rents. Rents would be controlled because the payments due under the master lease would be fixed for many years into the future. In negotiations, SOW would insist that the payments under the master lease be low enough that the co-op could rent out its 110 berths for $50 or less.

Becky also ventured gingerly into the issue of there being only 110 berths in her proposed plan, as opposed to 185 boats currently at Waldo Point. Using the previously conducted survey as evidence, she argued that not everyone at Waldo Point wanted to be part of a legalized marina, and 110 berths would accommodate the number who did. The new SOW co-op could not afford to get into the position having more berths to rent out than it could find takers. If it did, the co-op would default on the master lease, and the entire project would collapse.

Becky sat down, and the moderator asked for the hands of people who wanted to talk. Dozens of hands shot up. Then, apparently by prearrangement, the moderator called on Achille.

Achille struggled to rise from his mangy wingback armchair. Instead of climbing onto the platform, he stood in front. He slowly looked around, as if to gather strength to speak.

"I've lived in this community for eighteen years," he began, in a voice withered by age. "And all that time I thought I knew what sort of community this was.

"I thought this community was a place where people were trying to build a society that was different from, and better than, the world outside. A world centered on people — their happiness, their freedom, their ability to create and to love. As opposed to the world outside, where the only thing that matters is money — how to make it, how to grab it from other people, how to spend it in order to make other people jealous. I thought this community was a place where people cared for each other, not just for themselves. I thought this community was a place where people came to follow their dreams, not to make a real estate deal. I thought this community wanted to serve as an example to the world outside, not beg for a few of its crumbs.

"But apparently I was mistaken all that time. For now, a group of people from within this community has come forth with a plan, and they are seeking our endorsement of their plan. What they are proposing is that this community get into bed with as rapacious a real estate developer as one can imagine, and enter into a deal with this real estate developer that would divide and shatter this community into a group of privileged winners and a group of outcasts.

"Let me be specific."

By now the twilight had disappeared almost completely, and the only light cast was the restless flame of the fire, turning faces orange and casting them in silhouette. The audience was rapt, listening to Achille's oration in profound silence.

"This developer, this Strawberry Point Harbor Associates — and by the way, isn't that a ridiculous name? — this Strawberry Point Harbor Associates group is truly evil. They came to our community committed from the very outset to exterminating us. They never talked to us, never even showed their faces here. Instead, they conspired with the county to figure out the quickest way to get rid of each and every one of us. Yet now the proposal is to kiss and make up with this despicable group so that we can cut a real estate deal with them.

"And what would this deal provide? Basically, it would split this community right down the middle. On the one side would be a group of privileged people who would get berths in the developer's new, fancy houseboat marina, alongside all the rich folk. And on the other side would be a group of outcasts — people too poor, or who value their integrity and their freedom too much, to fit into the developer's plutocratic scheme.

"What would become of these outcasts? Why, they would have to go. And would SOW protect and defend these people — SOW, which was created to defend the waterfront community, each and every member, and not just certain privileged members? No, SOW would be standing alongside the county and the developer pushing these people out. For by logic, if you are saying that some, and only some, of our members should have the right to stay, you are also saying that the others must leave.

"I can't speak for anyone else, but I can speak for myself. If this nefarious plan ever becomes a reality, I shall be among the outcasts. I shall proudly be among the outcasts. For never will I hand over so much as one dollar that I know will eventually end up in the hands of a despicable group of capitalists so alien to this place they don't even know the difference between Waldo Point and Strawberry Point. I would hate to see this community split, but if a split is forced upon us, I know which side I shall be on."

With this, Achille shakily sat down. His girlfriend covered him with a blanket.

A lengthy silence followed; the crowd was obviously moved. Even I was moved, though most of the time I regarded Achille as a lecherous old goat whose politics were stuck in the 1930s.

The moderator next called on Kevin. "There seems to be a lot of misinformation around here. I want to set the record straight.

"In the first place, nobody's forcing anybody to do anything. You don't have to be part of the small-boat harbor if you don't want to be. In fact, the plan is based on the assumption that roughly one-third of the people here now will not want to be part.

"Second place, if the plan goes through and you don't sign up, you won't be any worse off than you are now. Sure, if the plan goes through and you don't sign up, you'll be illegal. But you're illegal right now. All of us are illegal. The small-boat harbor won't make any difference to your legal status. Illegal before, illegal after. No difference.

"So to the people who are opposing this proposal, I say, 'If you don't have to be part of the small-boat harbor, and it won't affect your legal status one way or the other, why are you so hell-bent on stopping it?'

"Achille just spoke about the values of this community. I thought one of the values of this community was respect for other people's differences. I thought one of the things we stood for was the proposition that everybody should be free to lead his life in his or her own way, and not have some groupthink or conformity imposed on him or her. So if some of us want to be part of a legalized marina and pay rent, and some of us don't, why not just respect that difference? Why not let each group do its own thing, instead of the no group saying to the yes group, 'We won't let you.'

"I for one look forward to being part of the small-boat harbor. I don't like dumping raw sewage into the bay; I want to have a decent sewage system. I don't like the fire hazard here; I want to live in a place that has decent wiring and fire safety. I don't like being illegal; I'd rather be legal.

"And one thing I'm not hearing from any of the opponents of this plan is any alternative. If not this plan, then what? Are we just supposed to keep on battling the cops, keep on getting arrested, keep on getting injured ad infinitum? To what end? Just to keep on battling and getting arrested and getting injured?

"Because the county and the developer are not going to give up. There may have been a lull for the last few months, while they figure out what to do about the Midnight TRO. But they'll be back, you can count on that. There's too much power and too much money at stake for them not to come back.

"Right now we're in a good position to negotiate, because the sinking of the Midnight TRO has been a big blow to the Strawberries and the county. That means we have leverage, and we may not have it in the future. It's the right time for us to negotiate, and I think we have a good plan. I urge everybody to vote in favor."

Kevin sat down, again to silence, though not the stunned silence that had followed Achille's oration. I thought to myself, a good case, well put.

The moderator next called on Hank.

Hank stood up and slowly mounted the platform. Lit from only one side by the flickering blaze, his face seemed even more a landscape of hollows and ravines, his eyes even more sunken, than ever.

"I'd like to begin," he said in his gruff voice, "by asking some questions of our attorney here" — he pointed at me — "Mr. Spenser."

A surge of adrenaline jolted me onto extreme alert. What did he want with me? Was he going to challenge me? Or honestly seek legal advice?

"Now Mr. Spenser, you represented Justin Lambert in his eviction lawsuit, didn't you?"

"Yes, the Owl case."

"And you won that, didn't you?"

"Yes."

"And ever since then, the Strawberries have been so scared they haven't even tried to evict anyone else, isn't that true?"

"I can't say whether it's fear or whatever, but it's true, ever since Justin won, Strawberry Point Harbor Associates hasn't brought any more evictions."

I felt a little less tense. So far Hank wasn't attacking me.

"And there's also our big lawsuit against the Strawberries and the county. I know it lost for the TRO, but the lawsuit itself is still there, right?"

"I'm not sure what you mean by 'still there.' It's still on file in the County Clerk's office, if that's what you mean."

"It's going to come to trial someday, right?"

"Well . . . , to bring a case that big with opponents that well-funded to trial would require a huge expenditure of time and energy. Speaking only for Marin Legal Aid, I don't think we could commit to that amount of time and energy unless we thought the chances for success at trial were reasonably good. And I'm not sure, based on the reaction we got when we went in for a TRO, that the chances for success in Save Our Waterfront v. County of Marin are all that good."

For a moment Hank said nothing. Then, "But it's still there, isn't it? It hasn't been thrown out of court, has it?"

"No, it hasn't been thrown out of court. While the judge denied our application for a TRO, there's been no ruling on the overall case."

"So even if you didn't want to work on it, or Marin Aid didn't want to work on it, some other attorney could come in and take over, right?"

"I suppose."

"Okay. Switching now to the Midnight TRO, to our own efforts, that seems to have been a pretty effective way of stopping them from constructing, wouldn't you agree?"

I paused and smiled. "I'm under an ethical obligation as an attorney not to encourage my clients to break the law, and arguably the sinking of the Midnight TRO was an illegal act. So I hope you'll understand if I decline to answer that question."

"Sure, sure. I understand. But you'd agree, wouldn't you, that the sinking of the Midnight TRO has stopped all construction for the last four months?"

Had Hank been watching old *Perry Mason* reruns? He seemed to have been practicing the art of cross-examination.

"That's obvious."

"Okay, now, taking all these things together — the win in Justin's case, the lawsuit we've got going against the county and the Strawberries, and the success we've had with the Midnight TRO — doesn't all that mean that our situation isn't desperate?"

"Desperate? No, I wouldn't call your situation desperate. Who's saying it's desperate?"

"Well, there's a lot of people going around arguing in favor of Kevin and Becky's plan by saying that if we don't do something soon, the world's going to come to an end. I'm just trying to show that's not the case."

"Actually, I thought I just heard Kevin make the opposite argument. He was saying that because SOW has had these victories recently, it's a good time to negotiate, SOW has leverage. That's the opposite of saying SOW is desperate."

Hank said nothing. Perhaps it was the harsh firelight on his rutted face and hooded eyes, but he seemed to be glaring at me.

"I guess you're hearing something different from what I'm hearing. What I'm hearing, and I'm hearing it day and night around here, is that we got to do something, we got to enter into some sort of deal, no matter how rotten it is, because we can't go on living the way we do now. And what I'm saying is, we *can* go on living the way we do now, at least if we all stick together and are willing to fight. Let me ask you, Mr. Spenser, don't you think it's entirely possible we could say no to this deal, or to any sort of deal, and still be here years from now?"

"I don't know how to answer that question. Years — how many years are you talking about? And there're so many unknowns. For example, in terms of evictions, we won Justin's case based on his particular set of facts. I don't know if other boats here have that same set of facts. And the Strawberries could try legal remedies other than unlawful detainer. They could try ejectment, or the county could try nuisance abatement.

"Similarly, in terms of protests, or Midnight TRO-type activities, I'm not the one to ask, you need to ask the SOW membership. How many times are they willing to get arrested to preserve the status quo? How many days are they willing to take off from work to protest? How many times are they willing to get maced? These are not questions for me to answer. They're for the SOW membership."

Hank stared at me. With his long, lank hair and shabby clothing, barely lit by the flickering fire, he looked like a potential mugger coming at me in a dark alley. I sensed, beneath his surprisingly articulate exterior, a deep current of anger.

"Thanks for your help, Mr. Spenser," he said at last. He turned from me to face the crowd.

I'd been dismissed. How had I performed? I thought I'd answered his questions fairly, honestly, and without openly favoring Becky's plan. But still I seemed to have pissed him off. Perhaps he was pissed off to begin with. What was he now going to say to the membership?

"I hope you were all listening to Achille," Hank said, "because he's the one we should all be listening to. Remember Achille was the one who made this place what it is. He inspired us, he led us with his wisdom and his understanding. I tell you — this man is a genius. He's one of the greatest thinkers of our time, and I don't think any of us can even grasp how much knowledge he has. And he's always been willing to share his knowledge, because he's the most generous person you can imagine. Even though he comes from the Byzantine royal family, he's willing to talk to anybody, talk to kids with nothing but the clothes on their backs, talk to guys with maybe something a little off in their heads.

"So what I'm saying is, Achille's the heart and soul of this community. Remember, when we had our election of officers, after we first started SOW, he was the unanimous choice to be president. Everybody knew then that the best way to maintain our freedom and protect our right of navigation was to follow Achille. It's the same now. To keep what we've got here going, we need to follow Achille.

"Now you all heard Achille talk a few minutes ago. I don't know about you, but when I heard him analyze this plan that people are pushing and heard him explain what going for that plan would mean, I said to myself, 'That's it. Exactly.'

"But there's one thing Achille didn't talk about. I don't want to talk about it either, but I got to. The sad fact is Achille's eighty-five, and his health hasn't been good this last year. He may not have much longer to live. And I can tell you one thing. If this plan goes through, it'll kill him."

Hank paused. Standing with his arms rigid at his sides, fists clenched, head bowed, he seemed about to explode. I looked over to Achille. His head too was bowed, his eyes closed.

"That's what makes me so fucking angry about this whole thing. We've got these people" — he moved toward Becky and Kevin and pointed a finger at them, actually more at Kevin — "who are newcomers to this community. They only got here a few years ago. Achille and I have been here for decades. And now these new people decide they know what's best for this community, so they come up with a plan that divides us down the middle and has one half paying money to the bloodsuckers that claim they own this place and the other half kicked out. It makes me sick to my stomach."

Hank turned back to the crowd. "Here's what it boils down to. Achille's worked his whole life to build up this community and teach it the right values. Now, when he's eighty-five and not got much longer to live, are we going to throw it all back in his face? Are we going to make him die of a broken heart? Is he going to die knowing that he failed?

"I just can't . . . "

Hank's voice faded to sobs. He slowly walked back to his seat and sat down. Once again, the audience sat in stunned silence.

I was as stunned as anyone else. I couldn't believe that Hank — tough-looking, even sinister-looking Hank, the gruff auto mechanic in his fifties — had delivered such a maudlin speech. Surely there were better arguments against Becky's plan than simply hero worship of Achille. What about the 47 percent of the SOW membership who in the survey had said they couldn't afford $50 a month in rent? *I* could certainly make an argument out of that. But Hank chose instead to stake everything on blind allegiance to Achille. What was going on between Hank and Achille anyway?

I also thought Hank's pointing a finger — literally — at Becky and Kevin and thereby making everything personal was out of line. Way out of line. His jab at them for being newcomers to the community proved only that we-were-here-first snobbery existed even at Waldo Point. And it was strange that Hank seemed to aim his venom more at Kevin than at Becky, when the true architect of the plan he hated so much was Becky.

Hank Foster, weird bird.

The April evening was growing chilly with the dense cloud cover turning to fog. All of us at the meeting were completely cut off from the outside world; reality for us extended only as far as the light from the big bonfire. People retreated further into their blankets and big overcoats. I zipped up my leather jacket.

The moderator next called on Montse. As she walked to the front of the audience, the metal and glass of her many necklaces and bracelets shimmered in the firelight.

"Everybody so far has talked about community, and I want to talk about that too. I've always said the best thing, the really important thing, about Waldo Point is our spirit of community. What makes this such a magical place is not our boats or the ocean or the views or the freedom. It's the people. Over the past few years we've done things together, learned from each other, helped each other, had fun together, had bummers together, told our woes to each other — all this as a community. And I love it.

"But a community can't be frozen in time. To stay together, a community needs to grow and evolve and change.

"There's one thing about our community here at Waldo Point that nobody has mentioned so far. And that is, we're all getting older. We're no longer a bunch of kids fresh from the Haight-Ashbury like we were a few years ago. We've built homes for ourselves, a lot of us have paired off, we have more at stake now.

"Did you know that over the past year we've had five babies born at Waldo Point? Five babies.

"Ryan and I have talked about having children. But every time we do we come up against the obstacle that we don't think Waldo Point as it exists now is a safe place to raise a child. We don't think it's right to raise a child where there's raw sewage everywhere. We don't think it's right to raise a child in a place with the kind of raunchy electrical wiring and fire hazard we have now. So every time Ryan and I talk about it, we come to the same conclusion. We can have children, or we can stay at Waldo Point, but we can't do both."

While Montse was speaking, I surveyed the crowd. Given the lack of light, the fog and the fact everyone was bundled up, it was hard to read individual faces. But definitely most of the crowd was young — in their twenties or early thirties. Young like Montse, Becky and Kevin. Not old like Achille and Hank. Montse was appealing to the right demographic.

"Of course," she continued, "you can say it doesn't matter if Ryan and I leave. Other people will take our place. But when I think of community, I don't think of a place where people come and go, where they spend only a few years as a way station to someplace else. I think of community as a place where people grow and evolve together, where relationships deepen over time, where people can build for a lifetime.

"As I said, Ryan and I love Waldo Point, we love the spirit of community here, and we want to stay. But we also want to raise a family. We think Becky's plan is our best hope to be able to do both, and we're looking forward to having a legal berth, with safe electrical wiring, and no raw sewage. That's why we're voting for the plan."

Montse retook her seat in the audience. There was none of the tension that had followed Achille's and Hank's remarks. Some in the audience talked to each other.

The moderator next called on Hashbury, the guy I'd originally called Mr. Tie-dye. The crowd relaxed. Things were about to lighten up.

Hashbury meandered to the front of the audience. The firelight brought out the red in his dreadlocks and the mélange of pink, yellow, lime green and lavender in his oversized tie-dye T-shirt. Once in front of the audience, he belched, and then began speaking.

"They say we gotta pay rent. Pay rent for floating on the Pacific Ocean.

"Sounds kinda weird to me. But hell, I'll go along with it. After all, I piss, and the ocean takes it away. I shit, and the ocean takes it away. Ocean works hard for me. Does all the dirty work. So I guess maybe I oughta pay something.

"But I'm sure as hell not going to pay anything to that Strawberry Point Assholes group. Who do they think they are, saying they own the ocean? Nobody owns the ocean. How *could* anybody own the ocean? It's . . . slippery.

"I'll tell you who I'll pay rent to. I'll pay rent to Neptune. He's the lord of the ocean, right? He's the one we should pay rent to."

People laughed, but probably would have laughed harder had the evening not been so tense.

Hashbury pointed an unsteady arm toward Achille. "Hey Achille," he said, "you should be able to help us with that. You must know Neptune through your old empire. You can set it all up for us."

Achille smiled benignly, apparently willing to forgive Hashbury his conflation of pagan Rome with the fervently Christian Byzantine Empire.

"So when this deal with Neptune's all wrapped up," Hashbury continued, "call me back and I'll sign up. Until then, it's like I've always said. Waldo Point's a paradise. We got drugs, we got girls, and we got rock 'n' roll. Man, what else do you need?"

For the first time that evening, a speaker sat down to applause.

The meeting continued another bone-chilling hour and a quarter. Most speakers favored Becky's plan. Dan Porter, the attorney, made an effective presentation in favor.

Opposing the plan, a few people stood up to say they couldn't afford fifty dollars a month in rent. But the number making that claim was fewer than I expected.

No one asked me any more questions. I sat with my collar up, my hands in my pockets, and still the dampness seeped through and I was cold.

When the meeting finally ended I tried to slip out without talking to anyone. I didn't want to be seen as overtly favoring either the Achille-Hank faction or the Becky-Kevin-Montse faction. But I immediately ran into Becky and Kevin and felt I had to say something.

"What did you think?" I asked, generically.

I feared the pair would be furious about Hank's attack on them, and hence I might be in for a diatribe. But instead Kevin grimaced and said, calmly and slowly, "I hope our membership has the ability to distinguish sanity from insanity."

Becky smiled in agreement, adding, "And if they don't, maybe they don't deserve to be saved."

The SOW membership was to vote on Becky's plan the next day. Polls would be open from 10:00 am to 6:00 pm. Results would be tabulated by 7:00 pm.

I gave Becky and Kevin my home number and asked them to call me the next night with the results. They agreed.

Becky called around 7:30 pm. SOW's membership had voted in favor of going ahead with the plan, by a margin of 132 to 62.

"Congratulations, I think it's definitely the right decision for SOW. It's also, I might add, a real feather in your cap. Not that there was anything the matter with your cap even before the new feather."

"Why thank you," Becky said, lowering her voice to its sexiest range. "And you're pretty rad yourself." I felt a tingle; it had been a while since I'd experienced Becky's flirtatious side.

"And you'll be glad to know," she continued, "you're going to be hearing from me a lot in the next few weeks. I intend to move on this thing as fast as possible and as hard as possible. And you're definitely part of the plan."

"That's fine with me. I look forward."

No need to fake that response.

22
THE STRAWBERRIES

Becky was true to her word. The very next day after the SOW election she called to say she'd set up a meeting with Strawberry Point Harbor Associates and wanted me to attend. She'd also tried to set up a meeting with the county supervisor who represented the district in which Waldo Point was located, but he was out of town.

The meeting with Strawberry Point Harbor Associates was to take place not at their own offices, but rather at the offices of their attorney, Lloyd Morgan, the nasty man I'd last encountered the morning after the sinking of the Midnight TRO. His offices were on the thirty-first floor of Three Embarcadero Center, a high-prestige downtown San Francisco office tower.

I arrived clad in my best suit and shoes — I'd recently bought a pair of good-looking Italian loafers. A high-speed elevator catapulted me to the thirty-first floor and opened to the law firm's lobby. The firm occupied the entire floor.

The lobby had off-white walls, hardwood floors covered here and there with heather Berber rugs, and select examples of modernist furniture spaciously arranged in an L shape. On the walls hung expensive contemporary paintings. I recognized — thanks to Tiffany I was becoming fairly knowledgeable about the art market — a Sam Francis and a Cy Twombly. The air smelled faintly of leather and ozone, the latter probably from the building's HVAC system.

I was the first of our group to arrive. Soon Becky, Kevin, Montse, two other women and another man arrived.

I was surprised at how demure and unsexy Becky looked. Wearing a loose fitting purple-and-black-striped sweater and black skirt, she looked as if she'd come to apply for a secretarial position.

The others too were dressed more conventionally than houseboaters usually dressed. Still, with their sunbaked faces, long hair and well-worn clothing, the Waldo Point group looked incongruous sitting on furniture of chrome and polished leather in a spare, modernist space. Like rumpled country folk coming to visit rich relatives in the city.

While the others seated themselves, Kevin came over, squatted down in front of me, and said in a hushed voice, "In case Hank tries to contact you, you need to know he's no longer a member of the SOW board of directors and is no longer authorized to speak on behalf of SOW."

"Oh?" I said, a quizzical look on my face.

"We don't want to go into all the details. Just don't talk about any SOW business with him."

I wanted to know more, but reminded myself that if the houseboaters didn't want to explain their internal squabbles to me, that was their right. "Okay," I said.

Assembled in the chic lobby, the seven of us waited for ten minutes past the time of our appointment. Then an attractive and elegantly turned-out secretary came and led us down a corridor punctuated, like the lobby, with expensive contemporary art. The corridor took us to a floor-to-ceiling glass wall, behind which awaited a conference room housing a large maple-top table and leather swivel executive chairs.

Entering the room, we all stopped in our tracks, transfixed. For the far side of the room consisted of another floor-to-ceiling glass wall, this one the exterior wall of the building, offering a jaw-dropping panoramic view of San

Francisco Bay. Spread out before us were the piers, the water, boats of all types, the Bay Bridge, Treasure Island, Alcatraz, Berkeley and Oakland on the other side of the bay and a cloud-dappled sky. All from thirty-one floors up. With nothing in the way to block the view. It was like seeing San Francisco through the eyes of one of its peregrine falcons.

So dazzled were we it took us a while to sit down. Eventually we organized ourselves into a tight grouping at one end of the maple-top conference table. The Strawberries kept us waiting another five minutes. At least now there was the breathtaking view to compensate.

When the Strawberry Point Harbor Associates delegation finally arrived, it numbered only two. One was Lloyd Morgan, the group's immaculately tailored but not particularly charming attorney. The other was the man I'd seen twice before with Morgan — young, fairly nondescript, always dressed informally, always seeming nervous. Today he wore a blue dress shirt and slacks, no jacket, and again looked worried.

Morgan and the other man seated themselves side by side at the other end of the oval table. Going around the room for introductions, we learned the other man, the nervous man, was Cliff Willis, managing general partner of Strawberry Point Harbor Associates. My earlier guess was correct.

"Let's get started," Morgan said, offering no apology for being late. "We understand you have something you want to show us. That's the sole reason for this meeting, and we're just here to listen.

"Before you start, though, I want to emphasize that by being here and looking at whatever it is you want to show us, we're not committing to anything, and specifically we're not committing to any sort of negotiations with you or your group. You asked for this meeting. We didn't. We're simply being polite by agreeing to your request.

"That having been said, why don't you go ahead?" He waived his hand generally in our direction, and I thought I detected a faint grimace.

Ignoring the less than gracious introduction, Becky unrolled her plan and began to talk. She first went over the physical aspects of the plan — the rearranged piers, the addition and subtraction of berths. Next she went over the proposed legal structure — a master lease from the partnership to SOW, with SOW renting berths to and collecting rents from individual boat owners.

Then Becky got into the economic aspects. She emphasized that while Strawberry Point Harbor Associates would be losing 40 market-rate berths, the new small-boat harbor would have 110 new berths. Admittedly the rents paid by the residents of the small-boat harbor would not be as high as those paid by the marker-rate tenants, but the greater numbers could hopefully make up for the lower rents. SOW could not guarantee that the rents from the small-boat harbor would make up completely for the loss of the 40 market-rate berths, but SOW was committed to making the negative economic impact on Strawberry Point Harbor Associates as small as possible. Notably, Becky did not mention that the SOW membership had been promised that rents in the small-boat harbor would not exceed $50 per month.

Finally, Becky pointed to the intangible benefits Strawberry Point Harbor Associates would gain from making a deal with SOW. SOW could deal with opposition to the project, work to prevent protests and obstructions, and coordinate the moving of boats that would be necessary for construction. She didn't make any direct threats that, without a deal, protests and sabotage would continue. She was too tactful for that. But the message was clear.

While Becky was talking, I watched Lloyd Morgan and Cliff Willis. The attorney seemed bored, disdainful. The developer appeared interested, if still nervous. At one point he took out a handkerchief and wiped his brow.

When Becky was finished, Willis looked to Morgan for a response. The attorney remained silent for a minute, fingering his Countess Mara tie.

"You've obviously done a lot of work to put this plan together," he finally said, somewhat cordially. "And we certainly appreciate that. The plan is very ingenious in the way it folds a net 70 more berths in without making it seem any denser.

"Unfortunately, it's too late. The project's already past the point of no return. We can't amend or change the plan at this late stage.

"Among other reasons, we've already signed lease-options with quite a number of new tenants. We'd have to give them their money back and restart the whole marketing program all over again from scratch. And go through the Department of Real Estate again, which of course would be a nightmare. So that simply isn't going to happen.

"I wish we could be more encouraging, but as you can see, we simply can't."

While Morgan was speaking, Becky's jaw dropped, and her eyes widened in disbelief. "You've already rented out a lot of the berths?" she said when he finished. "Nobody told us about this. We live there, and nobody told us about berths being available for rent."

Morgan shrugged his shoulders. "I guess not."

"Well, why not? Don't you think, since we're the people living there now, we should have been given at least the courtesy of being told there were berths for rent?"

Cliff Willis had his handkerchief out and was mopping his brow.

Morgan waved Becky off. "Look. We're not doing the marketing. The marketing is being done by a firm called Platinum Realty. If you have questions about the marketing, you should address them to Platinum."

"Platinum Realty?"

"There're in Belvedere. We can give you their card."

I'd noticed ads placed by Platinum Realty in the real estate section of the *I-J*. They always trumpeted ultra-high-end homes in Belvedere, Tiburon or Sausalito.

Becky was stunned speechless. I took the opportunity to raise a question of my own.

"You said you'd entered into lease-options with a number of people. I can see the lease part. But what are the options for?"

"They're options to purchase the berth."

"Purchase?"

"Ultimately we plan to condominiumize the project."

"You're planning to condominiumize Richardson Bay?" Kevin couldn't restrain himself.

Cliff Willis rubbed his brow furiously.

Morgan again shrugged his shoulders, his favorite form of body language. "Most of the houseboat marinas in Seattle are condominiums. They work very well."

And make developers a lot of money, I thought. But I said nothing.

At this point Willis put his arm in front of Morgan, and I thought I heard him say, "Let me, Lloyd."

He turned to us, arms forward, palms facing up, almost a surrender pose. "Look. We have to do what the county tells us to do. If the county were telling us to build your plan, we'd build your plan. But that's not what the county's telling us. They're telling us to build the old D. B. Luther plan. So that's what we're building.

"I'll be open with you. We've talked to the county about changing the old plan. We have our own problems with it, different from your problems, but still problems. But the county isn't even willing to talk about possible changes. As far as they're concerned, the project was approved, it's final, and they're not about to reopen the whole can of worms.

"So here's what we can offer you. Talk to the county. If you can get the county to change the plan, we'll do whatever the county tells us to do. But until then, we have to keep working on the basis of the old plan. That's what we can offer you, and I don't think you can ask any more of us."

All of us in the Waldo Point delegation looked at each other. Gradually it dawned on us we had achieved something major. Now we only had one obstacle — the county — not two. If we could convince the county to go for Becky's plan, Strawberry Point Harbor Associates would not be separately opposed. Smiles broke out. As Willis had just said, what more could we have expected out of this meeting?

We refrained from celebrating in front of the Strawberries. But once the high-speed elevator deposited us at the strange, concrete-enclosed third-floor podium of Three Embarcadero Center, all restraints were off. We all began hugging Becky, congratulating her on a significant step forward for her plan.

When I stepped forward for my hug, I wondered if I might get one of Becky's flirtatious treats. But I didn't, just a very happy business hug. I turned to see Kevin standing next to us, watching. But even without a frisson from Becky, it had been a very good day.

23
URGENT TELEPHONE CALL

For weeks Tiffany and I searched for an apartment we could afford. Our search taught us we could get more value for our rental dollar in northern San Francisco than in southern Marin County, and we ended up renting a place in the Richmond District, where Tiffany already lived. I would have the more difficult commute, by car over the Golden Gate Bridge. Tiffany could take the 38-Geary bus to her gallery downtown.

On a windy first weekend in May, Tiffany and I moved to our new apartment. On Saturday we moved my belongings from San Rafael to San Francisco. On Sunday we moved hers — not many, she was a minimalist — from the Outer Richmond to the Inner Richmond. We'd long dreamt of having a candlelit dinner our first night in a new shared home, and that night we managed to find a stubby candle and place it in the midst of our Chinese takeout. One thing I had to say in favor of the Richmond district: There was a decent Chinese restaurant on virtually every corner.

We'd also talked about the pleasure of making love our first night in a shared apartment, and even though we were bone tired from all the moving, we still had energy for that task. Our lovemaking was slow, passionate and meaningful. The ideal christening for our new love nest.

Monday morning I was late leaving for work. Everything I needed — to make breakfast, to clean up, to get dressed — seemed packed underneath boxes of other things. The morning commute from San Francisco to San Rafael — the first time I'd driven it — also took longer than expected. I arrived at work an embarrassing forty minutes late.

Awaiting me was a phone message from Montse, "Please call. URGENT. PRIVATE."

I slunk back to my office, hoping Sam wouldn't notice my late arrival. "URGENT," "PRIVATE" sounded ominous. And why was Montse the one calling me? Usually when SOW wanted something, it was Kevin or Becky who called.

Arriving at my office, I closed the door and dialed Montse's number. "Hello," she answered in a subdued voice. Odd, since she was usually so ebullient.

"Hi, this is Rick. You called?"

"Yes. . . . I have some really bad news to tell you. . . . Are you sitting down?"

I wasn't; I'd actually dialed the number standing up. But I immediately seated myself and answered, "Yes."

She was silent for a moment. Then, "This is really hard." I waited for her to continue, but again she was silent. Finally, "Kevin is dead."

Every cell in my body seemed to shatter and die. My mind went blank, my limbs numb. "What?"

"He was killed over the weekend. Murdered."

"Murdered?"

"I'm afraid so. Gunshot wound to the head."

I slumped over my desk. No, this can't be. People I know don't get murdered. This has never happened before. There must be some mistake.

"Are you sure?"

"Yes, I'm sure."

I took a deep breath in, let it out slowly. "Do they know who did it?"

"Not exactly. But . . . Oh God, this is such a bummer."

What now? Something worse?

"I need to back up. For several years, Kevin and Ryan, my old man, and another guy named Kenny Hyde, who I don't think you know, have cultivated a marijuana plot in the Mendocino National Forest. It wasn't a big deal. It was just a part-time job for them, a way to make a little money and still have time left over for something else. Kevin used it as a way to subsidize all the time he spent on SOW. Anyway, and here's the hard part, Kevin's body was found at this plot in the Mendocino National Forest."

A jolt of acid hit my stomach. Great. All this time I'd been representing a bunch of warring drug lords. Who were never honest with me about who they were.

"Now please, please, don't go jumping to conclusions," said Montse. "I know it sounds like Kevin was killed in some sort of drug war. But Ryan and Kenny both swear up and down that can't be it. They say everything at their plot was totally cool, totally copacetic. They didn't have any enemies, there hadn't been any threats, nobody was trying to take over their plot. They're absolutely convinced Kevin's murder has nothing to do with their pot operation."

So what? I felt like saying. Having your vice-president's dead body found in the midst of his pot plantation is not good PR, no matter what the backstory.

My head ached. A moment ago I'd been heartbroken at Kevin's death. Now I was reviling him.

"Okay, if it didn't have anything to do with the pot operation, who *did* kill Kevin?"

A long silence. Followed by, "We don't know."

"Sounds like you have your suspicions."

Another long silence. Finally, "Let's just say we don't want to make any accusations we can't back up."

"Okay. . . . I guess."

I wondered if they suspected Hank. Based on what I'd seen at the membership meeting, he harbored a visceral hatred of Kevin. And there was also the mystery about his no longer being a member of the SOW board of directors.

But was Hank capable of murder? I wouldn't have thought so up till now. But I suppose anything's possible. Should I ask about Hank? No, Montse doesn't seem to want to talk about the subject, and I shouldn't get into the business of accusing someone when I have no real proof.

"Is some government agency investigating the crime?" I asked instead. "Who investigates crimes in the Mendocino National Forest?"

"For a murder, it's the FBI."

I let out an agonized groan. "So now the FBI is involved in the whole thing?"

"I'm afraid so."

What a disaster. The number two person in SOW's leadership murdered. And at the same time exposed as a pot grower. The FBI involved. The newspapers —

"Has this been in any of the newspapers yet?"

"I . . . don't know. We just got the news late yesterday. I don't know if it would have had time to get into the newspapers."

"Is there any way we can keep it out?"

"Keep it out? I don't . . . I don't see how we can keep it out of the Mendocino papers. But I know the assistant editor of *MarinScope*. I could talk to her." *MarinScope* was the local paper in Sausalito.

"See if you can get her to hush it up. I hope you realize what a public relations disaster it'll be if this story becomes headline fodder. I can see the headline now: HOUSEBOAT LEADER SLAIN IN DRUG WAR."

No sooner were these words out of my mouth than I realized what I was doing. I was orchestrating a cover-up. Just like Richard Nixon.

"Yes, yes," answered Montse, a willing accomplice. "I'll do what I can."

Better not say anything more. I've probably said too much already. Either Montse got the hint or she didn't.

I thought of Becky. What a tragedy this was for her. Of all of us still alive, she had suffered the greatest loss. Poor, beautiful Becky.

"How is Becky?"

"Not good. You can imagine. She and Kevin had been together for three years and were like two peas in a pod. They were perfect for each other. Plus, there's ... shall we say, an unpleasant atmosphere around here right now, and it's very hard on her."

"Unpleasant atmosphere" sounded ominous. Should I probe? Probably not. The houseboaters seemed to tell me only what they wanted to tell me, and maybe it was best to leave it that way.

"Do you think Becky would welcome a call from me?"

"I'm sure she would. She thinks very highly of you. She's your greatest admirer."

Really? Really!

"But don't call right now. She's trying to get some sleep. She was up all last night. Call later today, like maybe in the late afternoon."

"Okay. Will do."

For half an hour after my talk with Montse, I remained shut in my office, door closed, telephone calls declined, incommunicado, trying to sort out my thoughts.

Kevin's death saddened me to the core. I liked the guy. He was bright, witty, cheerful, genuinely interested in making the world a better place. From my standpoint, he was a dream of a client, always responsive, helpful and reliable — qualities not always found in people who walk into Legal Aid. And from the standpoint of SOW, his leadership abilities, willingness to put in long hours and level-headedness were invaluable. Without Kevin, or more accurately, without Kevin and Becky, for they came as a team, SOW would be as capable of effective movement as Achille's rotting ferryboat.

Furthermore, I personally had no moral objection to marijuana. My only problem with pot, having tried it numerous times in college, was that I found it a poor cousin to alcohol. And if there was nothing the matter with pot itself, why should there be anything the matter with growing pot? We didn't criminalize brewers, distillers or vintners. We didn't criminalize manufacturers of cigarettes. Why should we criminalize growers of marijuana?

On the other hand . . .

I thought back to the attorneys' meeting that took place after Kevin, Becky and Hank's initial visit to Legal Aid. My fellow staff attorney Judith had picked up Kevin's application form, stared at it disdainfully, and said, "This guy is white, twenty-eight years old, and says he's unemployed and has zero income. I'll bet he's a drug dealer."

I now had to admit: She was right.

Judith hadn't even argued the point that Legal Aid should not be representing drug dealers. To her it was obvious. And unfortunately, the same point would be obvious to many others. Obvious to Marin Legal Aid's board of directors. Obvious to Judge Carl Daley, who was both a member of our board and the judge to whom Save Our Waterfront v. County of Marin had been assigned.

Saving the Waldo Point houseboat community was not, I now realized, the cause that was going to make my reputation at Marin Legal Aid. In fact, I should probably start worrying about job security.

But damn it, there were 324 people — *324 people* — almost all of them low-income, living at Waldo Point. Was Legal Aid supposed to stand aside and remain mute while 300-plus low-income people lost their homes and were driven from the county? Marin County, sometimes said to be the most affluent county in the nation, had few enough low-income people as it was. Some residents even regarded the whole idea of a Marin Legal Aid as superfluous, since there were no poor people in the county. Losing more than 300 low-income residents would devastate an already endangered population.

I got up from my desk, wandered to my window, and looked out, resting my elbows on the sill. A car was having trouble parallel parking into a small space.

Moreover, my thoughts ran on, was everyone at Waldo Point a drug dealer? Surely not. Even assuming 50 percent were and 50 percent weren't — a ridiculously high percentage, in my opinion — that still left 162 people untainted by the dread stain of drug dealing. Was Marin Legal Aid supposed to stand aside while these 162 "virtuous" poor people were evicted from their homes and driven from the county?

Maybe SOW had made a mistake in choosing one of its leaders. Maybe not. But a mistake involving one individual shouldn't be a reason to abandon a cause benefitting hundreds of others. Think about the forest, not the particular tree.

On the other hand . . .

Assuming I continued working for SOW, what now were our chances of success? Not good, if the discovery of Kevin's murdered corpse in the midst of his pot plantation hit the headlines in the Marin papers. Our meeting with Strawberry Point Harbor Associates had shown that the battle was now entirely political, a struggle initially for public opinion and ultimately for the votes of the five county supervisors. Having SOW prominently linked to drug dealing and drug wars was not going to win that struggle.

And how effective would SOW be absent Kevin's leadership? Would Becky remain active in SOW after this? Would she be willing to take over as the group's sole leader, no Kevin by her side?

I sat back down at my desk. I was supposed to call Becky late that afternoon. The thought filled me with both anticipation and dread. Anticipation because I liked Becky, admired her, was a bit — well, more than a bit — infatuated with her, and also because I hoped I could ease, if ever so slightly, the pain she had to be experiencing. Dread, because I had no idea what to say to her.

I'd before never experienced the death of a close contemporary. Sure, I'd experienced the deaths of two grandparents, and someone in the class below me in high school had been killed in an auto accident. But I'd never experienced the death of someone both close and contemporary.

What could I possibly say to Becky? "I'm sorry" and "Gee, it's so awful" were obviously inadequate. I didn't have the faith to say Kevin's death was all part of God's plan and we should just ride with it. Whatever I said should make her feel better. But what *would* make her feel better?

By now it was 10:30. An hour and a half into the workday, and I still hadn't done a lick of work. I needed to unseal myself from my cocoon and face the world.

24
TRYING TO MAINTAIN

It occurred to me I should tell Sam about Kevin's death. He was probably going to hear about it sooner or later. Best sooner, and from me. Fortunately, he was able to see me within ten minutes.

I told Sam more or less everything. I left out only my suspicions of Hank, my infatuation with Becky and my plan to call her late that afternoon. Sam listened silently, a resigned look on his face.

When I'd finished, he said, "You know, we went into this thing with our eyes wide open. We knew there was some shady business going on down there. From what you've told me, it's hard to know how this is all going to play out. Just keep me posted."

I breathed a sigh of relief. He hadn't said Marin Legal Aid should get out of the houseboat business.

"Before you go, though, you look sort of shell-shocked. You need to get out of the office for a while. Why don't you go take a walk?"

My first thought was — impossible. I had a welfare hearing that afternoon, plus an answer in an unlawful detainer to get out. Having already wasted half the morning, I didn't have time for a walk.

But then I thought, he's right. I am shell-shocked. I do need a walk.

Marin Legal Aid was located on the south side of San Rafael's pint-sized downtown, and the area to the south of our offices was residential. I chose to walk there.

Gerstle Park, unlike the typical Marin County neighborhood, was flat and filled with modest older homes, many of them Victorians. It looked Middle American, like something out of Indiana. Its value for me that sad morning was its quiet. There were virtually no cars on the streets, no pedestrians on the sidewalks. Most of all, no murders, no drug dealing, no internal strife. I could walk in peace.

I had lunch at an out-of-the-way Mexican restaurant where I wouldn't run into anybody I knew. By the time I returned to the office, I was, if not exactly in a happy frame of mind, at least no longer shell-shocked.

The welfare hearing that afternoon was a balm to my wounded conscience. The client was someone my colleague Judith would heartily approve of — a twenty-two-year-old single mother, black, residing in public housing in Marin City, on welfare. In other words, not white, not male, deserving.

Sheryl Godwin, the client, had tripped over the "man in the role of spouse" rules in the AFDC program and was about to be cut off. Fortunately, after three years at Marin Legal Aid, I'd become something of an expert on welfare law and had handled several "man in the role of spouse" hearings before. As a result, even with only a few minutes preparation. I was able to get Sheryl reinstated. She was immensely grateful.

But on the way back to my office from the Civic Center, I wondered how did I know Sheryl's "man in the role of spouse" wasn't a drug dealer? For that matter, how did I know Sheryl herself didn't do a little dealing on the side?

Back at the office I still had the unlawful-detainer answer to get out, plus several urgent messages in my slot. I thought about calling Becky, but decided to wait until all my legal work was done. It was 5:15 by the time I felt ready to call, and even then I stared at the phone for five minutes before acting. What could I say that would be appropriate? Not just appropriate, but helpful and comforting.

I forced my fingers to place the call.

After five rings, "Hello." Becky's voice, usually low and sultry, now sounded tired and slightly hoarse. I pictured her perfectly shaped oval face weighed down by sadness.

"Hello, Becky. It's Rick."

"Rick?" Her voice picked up. "I was just thinking about you. I was hoping you'd call."

I felt a glow inside. Montse was right

"How could I not call? I thought so highly of Kevin. And I want to do anything I can to help you get through this."

She sighed. "I'm so glad to hear that. I was worried you might be . . . you know . . ."

"No, no, Becky. I consider you a friend, and I considered Kevin to be a friend. That's completely apart from my legal work for SOW. And friends stick by each other in a crisis."

"Thank you so much. And I really need your help now because . . . Well, because things here are just awful." She began crying.

"I'm so sorry," I said, immediately realizing how trite it sounded.

She continued to cry. Then, "Rick, we need to talk."

"What about?"

"I need some legal advice."

"About what?

"I'm so confused, I don't know what to do. I need somebody to tell me — "

The line went dead.

This was a common problem with calls to Waldo Point, due to the community's happy-go-lucky approach to wiring. The protocol was to wait for the Waldo Point person to call you back; she or he would know best when the lines were working again. I sat hunched over my desk, staring at my clunky black phone with its four clear plastic buttons, waiting for Becky to call back.

The previous call hadn't exactly gone the way I expected. Becky hadn't said anything about Kevin. Instead, she'd talked about things being "awful" here, "here" meaning presumably Waldo Point.

Did it have something to do with Kevin's murderer? Did she feel threatened? Did she also suspect Hank, or was that simply my imagination? Or was Kevin in fact killed in a drug war, and now Becky was worried about the same gang coming after her? As minute after minute ticked by, I felt more and more tense.

Line one blinked. I punched the button. "Hello, Becky?"

"I apologize for that. Our shitty wiring here. Let me get to the point quickly before we get cut off again. I need to talk to you, and it has to be face to face. I can't talk about this over the phone, particularly if I'm going to be cut off every two minutes. Can we talk face to face?"

"Sure."

"Can you come by here tonight?"

"Tonight? Um . . ."

A red light flashed inside my head. Tonight was Tiffany's and my second night in our new apartment, our first night coming home to it from work. Tiffany didn't necessarily expect anything as romantic and erotic as our first night, with its candlelit dinner and prime lovemaking, but she certainly expected me home at a reasonable hour. I was already late as it was. Of all nights.

"Um . . . Could we make it first thing tomorrow morning?"

"Rick, I hate to be melodramatic, but I'm scared. I don't want to go through another night feeling this scared. You said you'd do anything to help me. This is what I'm asking. That we talk tonight."

Reluctantly, I reconsidered. Now that I was living in San Francisco, I passed right by Waldo Point on my way home. In fact, the community's dirt parking lot was directly adjacent to the freeway interchange. Talking to Becky in person at Waldo Point wouldn't take much more time than talking to her over the phone, and I'd been willing to do that. Why was I making an issue about meeting face to face?

Also, I'd said I'd do anything I could to help her get through this tragedy. Was I going to say no to the first thing she asked?

"Okay, I can drop by Waldo Point. I can leave here in about fifteen minutes, which means I'll be at Waldo Point around 6:15, 6:30. Where do you want to meet?"

"Thank you, Rick, thank you so much. You don't know how relieved I am. Where? Just come to my boat. Do you remember how to find it?"

"I think so. Okay. See you soon."

As soon as Becky hung up, I tried to call Tiffany. But by that time she'd already left the gallery. I had no other way to reach her. We didn't yet have a phone in our new apartment.

25
BECKY

Her eyes were rimmed with red; tiny white lines ran down her face where her tears had dried; and she lacked her usual rosy glow. Yet even in despair, she was beautiful. Indeed, her long pale face, large sad eyes and long golden curly hair suggested a figure in a Botticelli painting. Below her face, though, her clothing — an oversized grey sweatshirt and faded jeans — pointed in a different direction.

I'd expected to find others present and comforting Becky, but instead she was alone. We embraced as soon as I stepped inside her boat. She rested her head on my shoulder and held me tightly. The embrace lasted and lasted and lasted, until I felt the stirrings of an erection. Embarrassed, I pushed her away, feigning a need to put down my heavy briefcase.

The interior of Becky's boat came back to me. The wood stove and smell of smoke. The knickknacks — mosaic peace sign, abalone shell, chunk of purple amethyst — and the wall hangings — dream catcher, Winterland poster, family photos.

We sat down opposite each other at the same table on which, three months earlier, I had first seen Becky's plan for a small-boat harbor at Waldo Point. I noticed a glass half-filled with amber liquid. Becky caught my look and said, "I'm having Scotch. Want some?"

I was normally a beer drinker, but if any day ever called for the consolation of Scotch, this miserable day was it. "Sure," I said.

"How do you want it?"

"Neat will be fine."

She poured me an ample shot of Johnnie Walker.

"So Becky, what are you worried about? Why are you afraid?"

"I'm afraid that if I step outside the door of this houseboat, I'm going to run into the person who killed Kevin. And who might be planning to kill me."

"Are you talking about a specific person? Or just the general proposition that Kevin's killer could be anywhere?"

"I'm talking about a specific person."

"And that person is?"

She grimaced, as if not wanting to answer.

"Are you talking about Hank?"

She nodded. "Yes."

"Why do you think Hank killed Kevin?"

"Hank hated Kevin. You saw how he acted at the membership meeting. His finger in Kevin's face. Hank was totally psycho that night. And one thing you probably don't know is that the day after the vote on the small-boat harbor plan Hank attacked Kevin — physically attacked him."

"He did? What happened?"

"Kevin and Hank were having a very loud, very heated argument on one of the docks. All of a sudden Hank rushed Kevin. It took three guys to get him off."

"What was the argument over?"

"Kevin had called a meeting of the SOW board, and Hank claimed Kevin hadn't gotten approval from Achille. It was really stupid."

"So Hank was once again acting as Achille's champion?"

"Right."

"Was this attack the story behind my being told Hank was off the board and I shouldn't talk about any SOW business with him?"

"Correct. We held an emergency board meeting right after."

"I see. . . . Okay, adding up, Hank clearly hated Kevin, and he'd attacked him once before. Any other evidence against Hank?"

Becky thought for a moment. I in turn pondered her small nose, full lips and dimpled chin.

"Nothing specific. It's just that it was always obvious Hank hated Kevin."

"What about the drug angle? Is what I was told — that Kevin's body was found in the middle of a pot farm that he and two other people from here ran — is that true?"

"Yes, that's true. But I'm absolutely sure the killing had nothing to do with the marijuana business. That was actually the most tranquil part of Kevin's life. Lord knows he had enough conflicts, but they were all down here, all having to do with Waldo Point. Mendocino was where he went to relax, where he didn't have to deal with arguments and disputes. I think Hank killed Kevin in Mendocino, or killed him somewhere else and dragged his body to Mendocino, just to make Kevin look bad. That would be exactly like Hank. He's very, very devious."

"You said you were scared and dreading the night. Are you worried Hank will come after you?"

She gritted her teeth and nodded her head. "If he's crazy enough to kill Kevin, he's crazy enough to kill me."

"Are you here alone?"

"Actually, since I talked to you, Montse and Ryan invited me to spend the night on their boat, and I accepted. I'm a little less worried now."

"Good, good. .... Getting back to Hank, have you shared your suspicions about him with anybody from law enforcement? Have you talked to the FBI?"

"Not about Hank. I talked to the FBI when they called this number to see who would answer and to tell that person about Kevin's death. They asked me who I was and how I was related to Kevin. Once I told them, they asked me a few very general questions. Did I have any idea why he'd been killed? Did I have any idea who might have done it?

"I have to admit that about a tenth of a second after I heard that Kevin was murdered, Hank's face flashed in my mind. But what with the whole shock of having just heard about Kevin's death and now suddenly being questioned by the FBI, I could barely get a word out. I don't know whether it was a conscious decision or not, but in any event, I didn't say anything to the FBI about Hank.

"Now that I've had more time to think about it, I'm glad I didn't. Do you remember my telling you over the phone I'm confused? This is what I was talking about. I don't *want* to talk to the FBI. I don't *want* the FBI down here poking into all our lives and everything we do. That would tear this community apart. Even people who firmly believed Hank killed Kevin would hate it, even me.

"So I'm torn. I want whoever killed Kevin brought to justice, whether that person be Hank or somebody else. But I don't want to bring in the FBI or any other law enforcement."

I sighed and pursed my lips. No easy answers here.

At last I said, "I think you're right that bringing the FBI into this community would not go over well. Which means you're right, there's a real dilemma. But let me add one more complexity to the mix.

"I'm worried about all this getting into the papers. At first I was worried about headlines reading HOUSEBOAT

LEADER DIES IN DRUG WAR. Maybe now I'm more worried about headlines reading HOUSEBOAT POWER STRUGGLE ENDS IN MURDER. But either way, those are pretty sick headlines.

"And I suspect the more the FBI is bought in, the more information they have, the more active they are in investigating the case, the more likely it becomes that the newspapers will pick up on the case, perhaps in a big way."

Becky looked even glummer than before. She got up, retrieved the bottle of Johnnie Walker, and poured each of us another shot.

"Not a pretty picture, is it?" she said. Her voice was lower, huskier — and sexier — than ever, perhaps due to the Scotch. "Can I ask you a legal question?"

"Sure."

"How obligated am I to cooperate with the FBI? I mean, am I under any legal obligation to call them up and tell them about my suspecting Hank?"

"Um . . . There's something called misprision of felony. But if I remember correctly — and mind you, I'm not a criminal attorney; this is all just memories from law school — misprision of felony applies only to failure to report the commission of a crime. In other words, if you'd been the one who found Kevin's body up in the Mendocino National Forest, you would have been obligated to report that fact to the proper authorities; in this case, the FBI. But as far as I know, you're not under any affirmative obligation to help them solve the case."

Becky looked relieved. "Are you comfortable with what I'm talking about?" she asked. "Not volunteering any information to the FBI. At least for the time being."

I thought for a moment. Becky focused her eyes on me — her wide, green, finely shaped but tonight sad eyes, bordered by blond lashes and a perfectly arched brow.

"I guess so. I can certainly see where you're coming from. Also, to be honest, the evidence against Hank, at least at this moment, isn't overwhelming. Hank hated Kevin, and he'd physically attacked him on one previous occasion. By the way, in that attack, Hank just used his fists and body, right? No knife or anything like that?"

"Correct."

"Did Hank ever make any threats he was going to kill Kevin?"

She thought for a moment. "Not that I know of."

"Was Hank known for having guns, or at least one gun? Do you know whether he owns a gun?"

"I have no idea."

"See, that's the problem. There's evidence against Hank, but it isn't, at least to my mind, proof beyond a reasonable doubt, which is what you need for a criminal conviction. If the case against Hank were stronger, I might have qualms about your keeping quiet. But since it isn't, I guess I'm comfortable with what you're doing. Or not doing."

"Good. That takes one worry off my mind. And by the way, don't think that just because I'm not talking to the FBI it means I'm going to be sitting on my hands. I intend to be very active. I'm going to investigate this murder on my own, and I'll keep at it until the case is solved. Whether it's Hank or someone else, I'm not going to let Kevin's killer get away with it. I may not be chatting up the FBI, but I'm going to be busy."

"Okay, great. And if I can be of any help to you, please ask."

"I may just do that."

"But one other thing, Becky. What about SOW? Are you still willing to serve as leader of SOW? Are you still willing to lead the fight for the small-boat harbor?"

She leaned back, a grim but also calculating look on her face. She took a swallow of Scotch, put the glass down, stared at it, and with her hand swirled the liquid around. Her breasts, not large but finely sculpted, complemented her slender, supple, youthful body perfectly.

"I may not be acting like it tonight," she finally said, "but I'm actually a fairly tough cookie. What Kevin's murder has done is made me even more determined to push the small-boat harbor through. If Hank killed Kevin, and I think he did, part of my revenge will be seeing the small-boat harbor become a reality."

I'd never seen Becky's usually soft face so intense, or heard her voice so low and sexy. "Excellent! That's certainly good news for the people of Waldo Point."

"But let me ask *you* a question. Are you still available to help us? Legally, I mean. After what's happened and what's come out over the last couple of days? Do you have any problems with your office not wanting you to deal with us anymore?"

"I talked with my boss earlier today and told him everything. He didn't seem too upset, or at least didn't tell me to get off the case. And certainty I want to continue working for SOW.

"Or maybe that's too broad. Let me amend. I want to continue working for SOW as long as you're still active. Frankly, Becky, without you, SOW doesn't have much of a chance, and I personally don't like working on things that are sure losers. My willingness to stay in the fight is conditional on your being there too."

"And to echo, my willingness is based on your being there."

I smiled. "Shall we swear a blood oath?"

She laughed and picked up her glass. "Why don't we swear a whisky oath?"

We clinked glasses.

"I swear."

"I swear."

Once we'd downed our mouthfuls of fiery liquid, both of us lowered our heads and fell into silence. Time to consolidate thoughts, to reflect on things discussed or promised. Becky had set forth an ambitious agenda. Finding Kevin's killer, while steering clear of the FBI or any other law enforcement. Getting the small-boat harbor approved, despite what could be an avalanche of bad publicity arising from Kevin's death. And time and time again I'd promised to be at her side. What had I gotten myself into?

As these thoughts swirled in my mind, I heard a long moan. I looked up to see Becky crumpled over, her hands to her face, tears streaming from her eyes. "I miss Kevin so much," she said between sobs. "I feel so lonely."

I jumped out of my chair, sped around to her side of the table, and embraced her from behind. Wrapping my arms around her shoulders, I rested my cheek against hers, and felt a fiery heat where our skins touched. "Oh, Becky, I'm so sorry," I said, realizing at once how trite it sounded.

"He was only twenty-nine." She grasped my hands with hers.

"I know, I know." I desperately tried to think of something comforting to say. The best I could come up with was, "He was a wonderful person."

Becky continued to cry and to hold my hands. Then, without a word, she pulled my hands from her shoulders and placed them on her breasts! My hands sang like angels. My sex was granite hard.

Was she conscious of what she'd done? Had she acted deliberately?

As the seconds ticked by, I grew more and more confident she knew what she was doing. I began to caress her breasts, her adorable breasts.

I thought I felt her melt into my caresses. But was I simply turning wish into fact? Should I back off? Or did I have license to —

Suddenly my inner debate became irrelevant. Becky got up from her chair, turned to face me, put her elbows on my shoulders and her hands in my hair. Her movements bore the seductive blur of drink.

She had stopped crying. With one finger I traced white lines of dried tears running down her face. Then I leaned over and kissed her lightly on the lips.

She pulled herself toward me, so close our body parts — her breasts, my erection — pressed against each other. "Kiss me again," she said.

I obeyed her command, this time thrusting my tongue deep into her mouth. At the same time I slipped my hands under her sweatshirt and began massaging her torso, and coiled my leg around one of hers and squeezed our groins even tighter.

After twenty voluptuous seconds in this position, Becky leaned back, tilted her head toward the boat's small bedroom, and said, "Come."

I followed.

I had once before dreamt of making love to Becky, and wondered if I was dreaming again. Perhaps I'd fallen asleep earlier in the day, perhaps even before I'd supposedly journeyed to Becky's boat. Perhaps Kevin had never died. Perhaps the entire day I'd supposedly just experienced had been nothing more than a long and disturbing dream.

But I knew I was not dreaming. My earlier dream had been ethereal, like lovemaking in the abstract. This was intensely physical. Visceral. I smelled the wood smoke in the air, mixed with Becky's honeydew scent. I heard the sound of rock music in the distance, along with her moans of pleasure. Most of all, I felt her warmth, the softness of her skin, the slipperiness of her interior. It was not a dream. It was heaven.

***

In the immediate aftermath of our cathartic lovemaking I felt as though I were resting on a bed of cashmere under a sky of gold. But within seconds the sky began to cloud over, darken, then shudder with thunder and lightning. The cashmere turned coarse, thorny, painful.

My mind had shifted from emotional-sensory mode to rational-lawyerly mode. Once that shift occurred, I heard a loud voice demanding: *What did you just do?*

The answer was not pleasant. I had behaved badly. In good lawyerly fashion, I drew up a list of three bullet points.

First, I had grievously dishonored the memory of Kevin, whom I considered not only a client but also a friend. Within hours of the discovery of his dead body, I was fucking his former girlfriend. What sort of a jerk would do something like that?

Second, I had betrayed Tiffany, with whom I claimed to be madly in love. Question: What happens the first weekday night Tiff and I have the opportunity to share an evening together in an apartment we chose together and in which we live together? Answer: I'm out tomcatting. Again, what sort of jerk . . . ?

Finally, I'd almost certainly violated the legal profession's Rules of Professional Conduct. One of those rules, I knew, dealt with lawyers having sexual relations with clients. I couldn't remember exactly what it said, but what would be the point of the rule if it didn't prohibit exactly what I'd just done?

Three violations. Two of moral obligations. One of law. Appalling.

I looked over to Becky. She seemed to be asleep. At least, her eyes were closed.

I took stock of my surroundings, which I'd completely ignored in my rush to obey Becky's terse command, "Come." The double bed on which Becky and I rested took up most of the small room. Above the bed, suspended from the ceiling, hung a voluminous textile, blazing with pinks, golds and pistachio greens. It looked like something picked up at one of the Indian stores along University Avenue in Berkeley. A corkboard covered with innumerable thumbtacked photos, cards and newspaper and magazine clippings dominated the facing wall. A small window to the side offered a view of a neighboring houseboat. Dusk, I noticed, was giving way to night.

The rumpled bed emitted a strange mix of smells. There was Becky's summertime scent, but also something else, and with a jolt I realized that something else was Kevin. This was Kevin's bed. I was usurping his bed, to say nothing of his girlfriend. Guilt enveloped me even tighter.

Becky still had her eyes closed. I thought of slipping out without saying anything, but quickly rejected the idea. Becky and I needed to talk. About what we'd just done.

I brushed her cheek with a single finger. She opened her eyes and looked my way.

"I can't believe what we just did."

She smiled, eyes slightly unfocused. After a long delay, "Maybe we didn't."

I wrinkled my brow. What did *that* mean?

Then a possible meaning of Becky's three words came to me. A meaning not just possible, but also irresistibly self-serving.

"That sounds like a good idea, Becky. Why don't we just agree, the two of us, that we didn't do anything."

"I'll go along with that."

"And since we didn't do anything, there's no reason to reason to tell anybody anything."

"I'll go along with that too."

I felt better. Or did I? For the second time that day, I had agreed to a coverup.

How did I feel? On the one hand, physically, sensually, I felt enraptured. Becky and I were lying on our backs, nestled side-by-side, skin touching, her warmth infusing our cozy nest, enjoying post-coital lassitude.

On the other hand, morally, I felt yucky. I needed to talk to Becky, clear the air, reach some type of closure. Whatever that meant.

"I know we agreed not to tell anybody in the outside world about what we did tonight," I said, looking up at the pink, green and gold canopy suspended above us, "but we can talk about it between ourselves. I feel really guilty. Don't you?"

A long pause followed. It might have been only fifteen seconds, but given our intimacy, it seemed an eternity. At last Becky said, "I generally try to avoid using the word 'guilty.'"

Once again her words took me aback. And seemed to close the discussion before it even began.

I remembered I'd been due home hours ago. Tiffany was waiting; I was inexcusably late and getting later by the minute. My dallying in Becky's bed was scandalous.

Summoning all my will power, I managed to haul myself out of bed and begin dressing.

"Are you going to be safe?" I asked when ready to leave. "Are you going over to Montse and Ryan's right now?"

"I'm going to pack my toothbrush and a couple of other things and head right over."

At the door we gave each other a chaste kiss. "Don't forget," she said. "You promised that if I need help nailing Kevin's killer, you'll be there."

"Don't worry," I said, stepping outside. "I remember."

26
TRIP HOME

I wasn't exactly drunk, but I wasn't completely sober either. I struggled to keep my balance on the narrow gangplank that led from Becky's boat to the dock. Then, once on the floating dock, I seemed out-of-sync with its rolling motion. I was also contending with darkness, for in the absence of streetlights, the only available light consisted of random shafts from nearby houseboats.

After walking about sixty feet, I came to a dead end. Leaving Becky's boat, I'd turned the wrong way. Eventually, by trial and error, I managed to find my way out of the Gate Six maze.

When at last I stepped onto dry land, I breathed a sigh of relief. But I was severely mistaken. The worst was yet to come.

Darkness enveloped the Waldo Point parking lot. No overhead lights, no headlights, no moon, no stars. But I was not alone.

A large truck blocked one end of an aisle I needed to cross in order to get to my Mustang. Just as I entered the aisle, it switched on its glaring headlights.

At first, I was grateful. The truck, whether intentionally or not, was helping me navigate the murky, rough-surfaced terrain.

Then I started to cross the aisle. The truck gunned its engine and with a spew of gravel and dirt shot forward. With a shudder, I realized the truck was heading straight for me.

I ran fast as I could in my half-drunken, lead-footed state, escaping the aisle by only inches before the big truck blast through. Once on the other side, I crouched down beside my Mustang, well back from the aisle.

Was this really happening? I asked myself. Had someone just tried to kill me?

Yes, it was real. I was not hallucinating. Someone was trying to kill me.

Was it Hank? No, it couldn't be. While I was obviously closer to Becky and Kevin than I was to him, I'd always treated Hank and his opinions fairly. Or at least so I thought.

But only an hour ago Becky had said Hank was psycho. If that was the case . . .

The truck started backing up. It passed the front of my car, coming to rest roughly where it had been earlier, about forty feet to my right. Then, it angled itself toward me, its hostile, piercing headlights pointing straight at me.

I tried to see who was driving the truck. Was it Hank? But the headlights were so bright they blacked out everything else.

Staying crouched down, I snuck into my Mustang. But even surrounded by metal and glass, I was still in shock — trembling, sweating, breathing in shallow jerks. I needed to calm down. I forced myself to take a few deep breaths.

What to do?

The truck seemed to be waiting for me to pull out. If I did, would it try to ram me? The idea seemed berserk. If the truck had hit me while I was running across the aisle, it probably could have gotten away with little damage to itself. But plowing into a Mustang at full speed? Only a madman would try that.

Becky's words came back to me: Hank is totally psycho. I needed to prepare for the worst.

My first strategy was to try to outwait the truck. That strategy was a dismal failure. The truck didn't move. Its blinding headlights continued to assault my eyes, its rough motor continued to idle. I, on the other hand, became more and more nervous, more and more agitated as the minutes crept by.

I came up with another plan, based on an observation I'd made earlier. When the truck had backed up and then gone forward to aim itself at me, I'd noticed it was slow in shifting between reverse and forward. My Mustang's automatic shift was much quicker. If I was willing to take a risk, I might be able to capitalize on that advantage.

But it would require quickness and alertness on my part. Could I pull it off? I had too much alcohol in my system; I was tired, scared, sweating and trembling. But I took a deep breath and told myself I simply had to turn myself into a professional stunt-car driver.

I began to creep out of my parking space, a foot at a time, right hand glued to the gearshift. When I was about three-quarters of the way out, the truck lurched forward. Once again, it aimed straight at me.

I yanked the Mustang's fast-responding automatic shift to reverse and zoomed back into my parking space. The truck roared past me, striking only air.

Further down the aisle, the truck shuddered to a stop. After time spent shifting gears, it began to back up. I waited, my car now in forward gear.

As soon as the truck cleared the space in front of me, I darted out, turned left, and sped toward the exit. Behind me I heard an explosion of gravel — the truck trying to stop. When I reached the parking lot exit, I looked in the rear view mirror. The truck was still at the far end of the aisle, barely moving, if at all.

I ran a red light at Bridgeway and careened onto the access ramp to 101. I kept looking in the rear view mirror, but saw no truck. By the time I reached the crest of the Waldo Grade, I felt confident I was in the clear.

With the threat of losing my life to the malevolent truck removed, I thought I'd be able to relax. But in fact, my mouth was dry, my neck stiff, my head throbbed, and worst of all, I was still trembling. I had to grip the steering wheel hard to keep the car moving in a straight line.

From worrying about the murderous truck, my mind turned to worrying about Tiffany. What time was it? I looked at my watch. It was almost 9:00.

Where had the time gone? Answers came quickly: Lolling in bed with Becky. Trying to outwait the evil truck.

What should I tell Tiffany? What should I say I've been doing for the last four hours? Or the real question, should I tell her about my tryst with Becky?

The moral and upright thing to do would be to tell Tiffany everything — be completely open and honest.

But not tonight. I've already had enough drama for one day. I can think about it tomorrow.

So what *do* I tell Tiffany?

Actually, Tiffany didn't even know about Kevin's death. I'd been so preoccupied and depressed all day I'd never called her, or rather hadn't called her until after she'd left the gallery. I could tell Tiffany about Kevin's death, then say a group of us had held an emergency meeting at Waldo Point to try to make sense of the situation. With this story, the only thing I'd have to apologize for would be not calling her during the day. I could also garner sympathy by telling her about the attack in the parking lot. That should take care of things.

By the time I crossed the Golden Gate Bridge, navigated the Inner Richmond, parked the car, and ascended the stairs to our apartment, it was 9:20. Tiffany greeted me at the door. "Where have you been?"

I didn't answer. Instead, I ran across the living room — dodging unpacked boxes filled with all our material possessions — headed into the bedroom, and threw myself down onto the bed in fetal position, arms wrapped around my head.

"Rick, what's the matter?"

"It's a long story."

I proceeded to tell Tiffany my sanitized version of the day's events — Kevin's death, the meeting at Waldo Point, the incident in the parking lot. I apologized for not calling her during the day, and pointed out that once she left the gallery I had no way to contact her. I asked for her forgiveness.

She threw herself onto the bed, wrapped her arms around me, and said, "Oh Rick, poor baby. What a horrible day. I feel so sorry for you. And terrible about Kevin too. Do I forgive you for not calling? Of course I do; you had so much else on you mind. I just wish I could have been with you to help you get through this miserable day." She began kissing me all over.

Tiffany was trying to make me feel better, but in fact she was making me feel worse. She was so loving, so trusting, so generous in spirit. I was such a cad.

But disturbing as those thoughts were, I was too tired and mentally exhausted to pursue them further. I needed to collapse.

First, I took a shower. I wanted to wash off all the Becky before I went to bed with Tiffany. As soon as my head hit the pillow, I was asleep. In the course of a single day, and in bewildering sequence, I'd experienced shock, grief, ecstasy, guilt, terror and guilt again.

27
THE DAY AFTER

The next morning I deliberately slapped off the alarm, went back to sleep, and didn't get up until Tiffany was almost out the door. When I emerged, she smothered me in a hug. "You're not going to work today, are you? You need to take the day off."

To be honest, I hadn't thought about what I was going to do that day. Simply getting out of bed had been challenge enough. But I immediately heard myself say, "You're right. I'll call in sick as soon as the office opens."

At 9:00 I ventured outside, located a pay phone, and called Sam to tell him I wouldn't be in that day. When he asked why not, I gave him my sanitized version of the previous night's events. "Are you sure you're not playing with fire down there at Waldo Point?" he asked. I told him I had no plans to revisit the place, at least for the time being.

Once I'd gotten the day off, I called Becky. At 9:10 her phone rang unanswered. She was probably still on Montse and Ryan's boat. Several more trips outside to the pay phone ensued, until finally at 10:15 she picked up.

I told her about my experience in the parking lot. "It's Hank. I know it. He was around here all day yesterday."

"Did you see him?"

"I didn't personally, but other people did. People I trust."

"Does he have a big truck?"

"Yes, he most definitely does."

"Are you sure you're safe staying at Waldo Point?"

"No, I'm not sure at all. But I'm not going to let Hank drive me out of my community."

"Okay. I hope you know what you're doing. Hope nothing more happens."

"So do I."

I tried to think of something reassuring to say. But couldn't.

"What bums me out," I said instead, "is that the incident the parking lot last night was a horrible experience for me, and it was probably perpetrated by Hank, but we don't have an ounce more evidence against him than we had before. I can't add anything based on what I saw last night. All I saw were headlights. I saw a big truck, but not enough to give any sort of description. As for the driver, I couldn't even see him, let alone identify him. Basically, all my misery last night was for nothing."

"I know, I know. We need more evidence. I'm working on it."

I told Becky I was at home, unfortunately without a telephone — the installer wasn't due till tomorrow — but I'd call her later in the day to see if there were any new developments. Meanwhile, I told her to have a safe day.

These two necessary calls made, I decide to relax and enjoy myself for the rest of the day. Having survived attempted murder, I had the right to indulge myself.

Unopened cardboard boxes containing Tiffany's and my belongings covered the living room floor. I located the box containing my cassette collection.

The little plastic boxes brought back happy memories of college and law school, years when I didn't have to worry about warring clients, murdered friends or attempts on my life. I hadn't added much to the collection in recent years — I'd been too busy trying to become a lawyer — so for the most part it remained a time capsule of music I loved in the late 60s and early 70s. Miles Davis' *Bitches Brew.*

Moody Blues' *In Search of the Lost Chord*. Jefferson Airplane's *Surrealistic Pillow*. Janis Joplin's *Pearl*.

I put Pink Floyd's *Dark Side of the Moon* on the tape deck. Fortunately I'd reassembled my stereo system late Sunday afternoon.

Since I seemed embarked on a late 60s retro trip, I decided to complete the fantasy. I located the seagrass basket in which Tiffany kept her pot stash and paraphernalia, brought everything out, rolled a joint, and smoked it. If you can't beat 'em, join 'em, I thought as I inhaled.

No sooner had the tangy smoke filtered through my lungs than, like a seaside village engulfed by a tidal wave, I was overwhelmed by a feeling of guilt.

What had I done the night before? No getting around it, I had acted despicably. I'd cheated, lied, and worst of all, I'd gotten away with it. Indeed, I'd actually profited from my misdeeds, for the story I told Tiffany — the one that left out the evening's most memorable event — had made her more sympathetic and affectionate than ever.

I was surprised at the weight of guilt I felt, even granting marijuana's tendency to exaggerate. After all, I'd had girlfriends before, quite a few of them, and hadn't always been faithful. And when I did cheat, I never felt particularly guilty about it.

Something had changed. With Tiffany, things were different.

And Becky? What about Becky?

Well, . . . she was beautiful, she was smart, and she was — I could personally attest to this — great in bed.

But Becky and I could never be a couple. I couldn't live at Waldo Point; she couldn't flourish anywhere else. Plus, I wouldn't want a long-term relationship with someone as flirtatious as Becky seemed to be.

Tiffany and I, on the other hand, already *were* a couple; our relationship was working, working well. This relationship was my best chance, perhaps my only chance, for a lifetime commitment. I should look upon it as precious, something to be carefully cultivated and protected.

Yet last night, I had grievously damaged it. Maybe Tiffany wasn't aware of the fact, but I was.

Should I tell Tiffany exactly what had happened, beg her forgiveness, and throw myself at her mercy?

Tiff and I had always talked about how we wanted complete honesty in our relationship. By that criterion, the answer was yes.

On the other hand . . .

Things between Tiff and me were pretty damn good as things stood. She'd been so gentle and loving and soothing the previous night, so sweet at our morning parting. Telling Tiffany about my unfaithfulness was never going to improve our relationship. And it could very well damage it. Why take the risk? Why poke at a skunk with a stick?

Okay, if not by confession, how could I undo the damage, make things right? I looked around. Where to start was obvious.

Aided by the single-mindedness that pot often fosters, I set to work, first reconstructing our concrete-block-and-board bookcases, then putting all our books on the shelves, finally tackling all the rest of the unpacking. By one o'clock I'd completed our move-in, leaving only a pile of empty cardboard boxes in the kitchen for later disposal.

After grabbing a quick lunch at the corner Chinese restaurant, I returned to the phone booth and called Tiffany. She was relieved to hear I was faring well and suffering no ill effects from the previous night. I told her I'd be waiting at the door when she came home that evening, plus I had a surprise for her.

With the rest of the afternoon open, I decided to hit a bar. Finding a bar in the Inner Richmond wasn't hard; Geary Boulevard had about six on every block. I ended up in a large, very Irish place, Pat O'Shea's Mad Hatter. There I settled into a Guinness, hoping to add the exhilaration of alcohol to the mellowness of pot.

But from where I was sitting, I couldn't help overhearing a nearby conversation. "My property taxes went up twenty-two percent last year," one man was saying. "Twenty-two fucking percent." He was a large man, older, probably retired, with white hair and a pink, fleshy face. Most of the other denizens of the Mad Hatter that Tuesday mid-afternoon met more or less the same description.

"Those damn government bureaucrats are getting a twenty-two percent raise, but my Social Security sure as hell ain't going up twenty-two percent," another man responded loudly. "You know what Social Security went up last year? Six percent. So my taxes are up twenty-two percent, and my income's up six percent. Damn, that thing had better pass."

"That thing" was Proposition 13, the property-tax-slashing initiative on the ballot in exactly four weeks.

"They should just fire two-thirds of those government bureaucrats," a third man said. "You'd never notice the difference; they don't do anything. That way you could give the third that was still there their twenty-two percent raise and still have money left over."

This conversation made me feel queasy. I was against Proposition 13. For one thing, I was a renter; I didn't pay property taxes, at least directly. More important, Marin Legal Aid received part of its funding from the County of

Marin, and word was that if Proposition 13 passed, the county, faced with huge financial problems, would eliminate — not reduce, but completely eliminate — our funding. In other words, Proposition 13 was a threat to my salary.

I slipped out after only one beer.

I next looked for a florist and found one immediately. The shopping convenience of the Inner Richmond was amazing. Surrounded by sweet-smelling floral magnificence, I bought a dozen red roses.

On the way home I stopped by the pay phone that had quickly become an integral part of my life and called Becky. "Any news?"

"Just one thing. We're putting on a celebration of Kevin's life — not a funeral, but a celebration — this Saturday, starting at four. It'll be in that area beside the parking lot where we had the membership meeting. And of course you're invited."

"In the parking lot? Um . . . After my experience last night, I have very little desire to return to the Waldo Point parking lot."

"Oh don't worry. It's going to be very safe. We're going to have guys stationed at various points around the parking lot keeping watch. And the event starts at four, so there'll be plenty of daylight. It won't be dark like it was for you last night.

"Plus, I think it's highly unlikely that Hank, assuming it's him, will strike in a place where there are a lot of people around. That's not his style. As far as I can tell, his style is to do things when there are no witnesses around. That was his style with you, and I'm convinced it was his style with Kevin too."

"You're probably right. By the way, is Hank still around?"

"I hear he is. I hear he goes over to the *San Rafael* every day and spends hours with Achille. But don't worry, everything's going to be very safe on Saturday."

"Okay. I guess I'll be there."

"Good. And bring your delightful girlfriend. What was her name? Tammy?"

I shuddered. This was not going to happen if I had any say about it, which I did. I did not want the two poles of my emotional life to meet.

"I'll ask her, but it may be a hard sell. She was really freaked out when I told her about what happened to me in the parking lot. She was always a little scared of Waldo Point — it's so different from what she grew up with — and now I think she's even more scared."

"Really? That's strange. She didn't seem scared that night on the Midnight TRO when we shared a joint. . . . Oh well, if she's scared now, it's your job to talk her out of it and get her here on Saturday. So we'll see both of you, right?"

"Right."

When Tiffany came home that evening, I greeted her with an enthusiastic embrace and fresh-tasting kiss, having just brushed my teeth. Her eyes widened when she looked into the living room and saw all the unpacked boxes gone, the bookcases assembled and filled, and all our belongings put at least somewhere. When she looked at me with gratitude, I handed her the dozen red roses.

I felt a little less guilty.

28
CELEBRATION OF LIFE

I ended up taking Tiffany to Kevin's celebration after all. After thinking it over, I decided my initial reaction — not wanting the two poles of my emotional life present at the same time and place — had been based on a faulty premise. There weren't two poles to my emotional life. There was only one — Tiffany. Becky was simply a business acquaintance, a very good business acquaintance to be sure, but still only a business acquaintance. If Tiffany and I were a couple, we should be able to socialize together with my business acquaintances. There was therefore no need to make a fuss about bringing Tiffany to an event at which Becky would also be present.

I'd feared for Tiffany's and my safety in returning to the notorious — at least to me — Waldo Point parking lot. But as it turned out, Waldo Point on the day of the celebration could hardly have seemed safer. A bright sun shone overhead, and attendees filled the lot.

Becky had called beforehand to say the dress code for the event was "festive," and Tiffany and I had donned what we thought were cheerful outfits. But immediately we realized we were among the most drab. People were dressed extravagantly, as if for a costume party — a Roaring Twenties costume party.

We wandered toward what seemed the center of activity. The thick air bore more fragrances than needed — beer, burgers, cigarette smoke, pot smoke, perfume, salt water, sewage. There were already at least two hundred, probably more like three hundred people gathered.

Montse rushed up. She wore a pink satin shift dress, a long white faux-fur stole and a red beret. Her arms and neck were draped with bracelets, armlets and necklaces that looked fabulously expensive but almost certainly weren't.

I introduced her to Tiffany. After they exchanged small talk, Montse turned to me and pulled out a newspaper. "Do you remember asking me to do something about the news coverage of Kevin's death? Well, here's what I was able to accomplish." She handed me a copy of *MarinScope.* Marked in red was an item that read:

"Kevin Cassidy, 29, of Waldo Point, died over the weekend as the result of a fall in the Mendocino National Forest, where he had gone camping. A celebration of his life will be held at Waldo Point at 4:00 pm this Saturday."

I smiled as I handed the paper back to Montse. "Good work."

"Thanks. I was happy with it too."

Montse turned to both of us. "Here's the skinny on this party. The purpose is to have fun. We decided that since Kevin was a fun guy, the best way we can commemorate him is to put on an event where we all have fun. So those are your marching orders — have fun."

She pointed toward a knot of people. "Becky's over there. Go see her, but first, get yourselves some beer or wine."

We heeded Montse's advice and headed to the bar. While we were there, Becky came over. She wore a 1920s-style low-cut cocktail dress that in texture was satiny and slinky and in color an iridescent mix of silver and blue, like sunlight reflecting off an azure sea. Draped over her shoulders was a chiffon wrap of the same elusive color, and in the center of her amply exposed bosom rested a heart-shaped silver locket.

"Rick, welcome to the party," she said, opening her arms in preparation for a big hug.

I edged warily into the hug and drew back as soon as politeness allowed. I then reintroduced Becky and Tiffany. They hugged and greeted each other like long lost friends.

"What a beautiful dress," Tiffany said.

Becky stepped back, lifted her iridescent gown, and curtsied. "You like?"

"Definitely."

"I have a question," I said. "I see all these amazing dresses you and Montse and lot of the other women here are wearing. Where do you get these things? How do you afford them?"

"I gather you haven't heard about Waldo Works."

"No."

"Okay. About twenty of us, all women from Waldo Point, operate a vintage clothing store called Waldo Works. It's along the road that goes from Gate Six to Gate Five. We've been in business several years and have developed a good reputation, so we get some amazing stuff. And of course, we always scarf off the best for ourselves."

"I see. Very clever."

"Thank you." She smiled proudly.

"Now Rick and Tiffany," Becky continued, "I want above all else that you enjoy yourself this afternoon and have a good time. That's the whole point of this event. But if I could delay that for just a few minutes, and Tiffany, if I could take your handsome boyfriend away from you during that time, I have some very important business I need to discuss with him."

I wasn't happy, either about Becky referring to me as "your handsome boyfriend" or about the proposition that, only minutes after Tiffany and I had arrived at the party, I would be leaving Tiffany by herself and heading off with

Becky. I was trying to think of a polite way to decline when I heard Tiffany say, "Sure. That's fine."

Becky said to me, "Let's go over there," and motioned with her hand to an area away from the crowd. I followed, looking back over my shoulder to Tiffany with a look that, I hoped, conveyed helplessness and resignation. Tiffany looked unperturbed.

Once Becky and I were outside earshot of the crowd, she became all business. "I heard from the FBI yesterday," she said in a low voice — low even by her standards. "They say Kevin was not killed in the Mendocino National Forest. They say their forensic evidence shows that he was killed elsewhere and transported there. As far as they're concerned, the only crime committed in the Mendocino National Forest was something called improper disposal of a corpse.

"They then say — and I hope I'm getting this right, it's a little confusing — they say the FBI investigates only *felonies* committed in national parks, and improper disposal of a corpse isn't a felony, it's a misdemeanor. So the FBI is bowing out of the case. They're turning it over to the United States Park Police, who are the ones who handle misdemeanors. Does all that make sense?"

"Yes, it makes sense, and that is news."

But despite the importance of Becky's news, I was finding it hard to focus. Discussing improper disposal of a corpse with someone dressed like a character out of *The Great Gatsby* was too bizarre. I needed to concentrate on what Becky was saying, not how she looked.

"Is there any indication how rapidly or how thoroughly the Park Police will investigate?"

"I was told, off the record, the Park Police only have something like two investigators for all of Northern

California. So they probably won't get around to even opening the file."

"Really? In other words, as a practical matter, nobody from the federal government is investigating Kevin's death anymore?"

"That's it in a nutshell."

"What about the Marin County Sheriff's Department?"

"What about them?"

"Are they investigating Kevin's death?"

"I certainly haven't asked them to, or even reported Kevin's death to them. And I don't intend to do so in the future. Don't you remember that as recently as last December all of us here at Waldo Point were engaged in war with those thugs?"

"So as a practical matter, no law enforcement agency at any level is investigating Kevin's death? Is that what you're saying?"

"Basically, yes."

I needed time to take all this in. I'd always assumed that if someone was murdered, it was the obligation of *some* governmental agency *somewhere* to investigate. But apparently not. Did this mean Hank, if it was Hank, had committed the perfect crime? Better not share that thought with Becky; it was too depressing. Of course, Becky was probably happy having law enforcement out of the picture.

"Doesn't this mean you got what you wanted? No law enforcement people down here snooping around and asking questions."

"I guess so. I suppose I was hoping the FBI would find Kevin's killer by investigating things elsewhere, like in Mendocino, just not here. But that was probably a pipe dream. To be honest, I don't think you can solve Kevin's murder without knowing what was going on here."

"You're probably right. . . . But as far as there being no official investigation going on anymore, remember the old proverb: Beware of what you wish for — "

" — because it may come true," Becky interrupted. "I know, I know. But let me point out something else about the FBI's conclusion. Their finding that Kevin wasn't killed in the Mendocino National Forest, that he was killed elsewhere and transported there, points the finger even more strongly at Hank.

"In the first place," she continued, "it blows away whatever was left of the theory that Kevin was killed in a drug war. That was what his killer was trying to make it look like, but it was a complete lie.

"Second, it shows that Kevin's murderer not only wanted to kill Kevin, he also wanted to make Kevin look bad, he wanted to ruin Kevin's reputation. And that fits Hank to a T."

Again I needed time to absorb what Becky said. The raucous sounds of people enjoying themselves filled my ears, and Becky's shimmering blue dress filled my eyes. Murder. Strange subject to be discussing at a party.

"I think you're right on all counts," I finally said. "But it still isn't what the law would call proof beyond a reasonable doubt. In other words, we couldn't just gather together everything we have now, take it up to the Marin County District Attorney, and say, 'Here's everything you need to get a conviction. You don't need to investigate any more. Just arrest the guy and try him.'"

"I agree. And that's why I'm working day and night to come up with more evidence. And I will come up with more evidence. Which reminds me, I hope you remember you promised that if I needed help in finding Kevin's killer, you'd be there."

"I remember."

"Good. Don't forget that. But now I have to get back to the party. After all, I'm more or less the hostess." Without offering a hug or an embrace, she headed off.

I hurried back to Tiffany, who seemed perfectly content observing the partygoers and their fanciful costumes. Together we migrated toward an improvised platform on which a band — the Redlegs, Waldo Point's house band — was setting up. I remembered the band's beanpole female vocalist, the deliciously named Maggie Catfish.

Once the Redlegs finished setting up, one of them stepped to the mike. "Welcome everybody," he said, until squawks from the sound system drowned him out. After five minutes of repairs and testing, he began again.

"Welcome everybody. We're all here today to celebrate and honor the life of one of our own, one of the very best of our own, Kevin Cassidy."

A loud roar from the crowd.

"We all have our own memories of Kevin, and different folks would remember different things. But there's one thing we could all agree on, and that is Kevin liked having fun, and liked seeing other people have fun. So the best way we can celebrate Kevin's life today is for everybody to have fun."

An even louder roar erupted from the crowd, and the Redlegs began to play. Soon couples began dancing, even though the only available dance floor was gravel and dirt.

Tiffany and I danced a bit, despite the difficult footing. We also had more to drink, observed the fanciful costumes, and joked around with strangers.

I insisted we leave before dark. Memories of my nighttime experience in the Waldo Point parking lot were still too raw to allow a stay beyond sunset.

We hunted for Becky to say goodbye. When we found her, she'd changed; she seemed unsteady on her feet and was slurring her words. She held a paper cup in one hand. I couldn't see what was in the cup, but suspected it was more than beer or wine.

"Sorry, but we have to be going," I said.

"Oh no. You can't go now. The party's just getting started."

"I know, I know. But we have a big event we have to go to tonight with Tiffany's family. Duty calls."

I leveled a knowing look at Tiffany. This was a little white lie we'd concocted earlier.

Becky sagged and looked grief-stricken. "Oh. . . . That sounds horrible."

Suddenly she lurched toward me, flung an arm around my shoulders and neck, and tilted her head next to mine. "We've been through a lot together, haven't we Rick

I froze. Yes, Becky, we've been through a lot together, but I don't want a full review in front of Tiffany. Particularly not the part about our recent lovemaking.

"That's right. But let's not focus on the past. Let's focus on the future. We're going to nail the goon that killed Kevin and attacked me. And we're going to turn your small-boat harbor plan into a reality. Isn't that right?"

Becky took a moment to think. Watching us, Tiffany looked unsure. Finally Becky answered, "I fucking hope so."

I extricated myself from Becky's embrace, took Tiffany's hand, and began leading us away. "Thanks for the great party," I said to Becky over my shoulder. "See you soon."

Like vampires in reverse, Tiffany and I escaped the Waldo Point parking lot before sunset.

29
NO NAME BAR

Becky called midafternoon. "Hi Rick. I have a very important and urgent request to make of you. Can you meet me at six o'clock this evening at the No Name Bar in Sausalito? As I said, it's really important."

"Um . . . "

I thought back to the last time I'd dropped by to see Becky on my way home from work. At the time I'd enjoyed the experience immensely, but later I'd come to regret it immensely. Plus, meeting Becky at a bar didn't sound very business-like.

On the other hand, I'd promised Becky that if she needed help in tracking down Kevin's killer, I'd be at her side. Promised her several times.

"Does this have to do with Kevin's murder?"

"Yes, it does."

This was the first time she'd asked me to make good on my promise. Was I going to say no the first time?

"Okay, I'll be there. But do you want to tell me why it's so important? And why the No Name Bar?"

"It's important because I'm hoping a certain person will show up and say in front of you what he's already said in front of me. If that happens, we can discuss what to do next. As for the No Name Bar, this certain person and I didn't want to meet with you at Waldo Point or any place too near. He likes the No Name, and so do I, so we agreed on that. Is it okay with you?"

I'd never been to the No Name Bar but knew it by reputation — as a dive bar and hangout for musicians, cherished for its open-mike policy.

"Sure. You're not going to tell me the name of this certain person?"

"It's not anybody you know. If he shows up, you'll learn his name. If he doesn't, I'll apologize profusely for wasting your time."

"No need for that. I'll be there."

After hanging up I immediately called Tiffany to warn her I might be late.

I arrived at the No Name Bar exactly at 6:00. The air inside the narrow space smelled of beer, cigarette smoke and nostalgia. With its battered wood furniture and memorabilia-filled walls, the No Name looked lived in, to say the least, but at the moment was largely empty. I easily spotted Becky siting by herself at a corner table backed by dark wood wainscoting.

She didn't offer a hug or even get up out of her chair to greet me. Instead, she sat with her arms on the table, a grim expression on her face, her usual springtime glow missing.

"He isn't here yet, but let's wait a while. He's not the most organized person in the world, and it wouldn't be unusual for him to show up late."

"Is he safe? I mean, should we be on guard?"

"He's safe. Don't worry about that."

We each ordered a beer and waited. Becky told me the celebration of Kevin's life had been a rollicking success, the party having gone on till after midnight. I asked whether Hank was still visible at Waldo Point. Becky said he was, but the only times he seemed to leave his boat were his daily visits to Achille.

Once she'd provided these updates, she didn't seem in a mood to talk. I tried bringing up a couple of subjects, but she didn't respond. Our beers arrived; she simply stared at hers. I'd previously seen business-like Becky and flirtatious Becky. Now I was seeing subdued Becky.

After a while I turned my attention to the memorabilia crowding the No Name's walls — Giants and 49ers pennants, rock concert posters, autographed photos, paintings by local artists, faded views of old Sausalito. Finally, at 6:15, a painfully thin young man with frizzy black hair sticking out in all directions and a cigarette dangling from his lips peered into the No Name. Becky signaled to him and he came over. "Rick, this is Lenny Rockman. Lenny, this is Rick Spenser, the attorney I was telling you about."

"Hi, Lenny. You from Waldo Point?"

"Yeah." We shook hands, and after taking a deep drag from his cigarette, Lenny sat down.

Becky ordered Lenny a beer, then said, "Okay, Lenny, what I'd like you to do is tell Rick what you told me about overhearing Hank Foster."

"Okay," he said, sounding like he didn't really want to. Turning to me, he said, "I was having a drink at the B Street Tavern in San Rafael — "

The B Street Tavern in San Rafael. It was only a couple of blocks from our Marin Legal Aid offices; I walked by it every day. But I'd never been inside. From the street it looked fairly sleazy, and at night I'd often noticed police cars parked in front.

" — and I happened to be sitting at the bar next to Hank. He was juiced to the max. Man, he was totally wasted."

Lenny Rockman pulled out another Camel and lit it with the burning tip of his previous smoke. Ever since he sat down, he'd been jiggling a foot.

"Anyway, Hank was talking to Ernie Jordan on his other side, and Hank was so sloshed he was talking real loud, practically shouting, so I could hear everything he said. After a while I heard him say, 'You ever used a silencer on a gun?'

"And Ernie says, 'No, can't say I ever have.'

"Hank says, 'Well then let me tell you. It's the greatest thing since sliced bread. If you catch my drift.'

"Ernie says, 'Really? How so?'

"Hank says, 'With a silencer, you can do any fucking thing you want with a gun and get away with it.'

"Ernie don't say nothing, so Hank says, 'You don't believe me, do you?'

"'I believe you,' says Ernie.

"But Hank ain't listening, so he goes on. 'Give you an example,' he says. 'There was this guy. I hated his guts. A real phony, all full of himself. So one night, late at night, I waited for him where I knew he'd be pulling in with his car. When he got out, I grabbed him from behind, put my hand over his mouth, and fired into his head point blank.

"'Now here's the amazing part. With the silencer on, there weren't no noise. No noise at all. There was probably a hundred people within a quarter mile of where I'd offed the fucker, and nobody heard a damn thing.'"

Becky visibly cringed at the words, "fired into his head point blank." I felt queasy myself.

Lenny continued his narrative. "So Ernie says, 'Yeah, that's great. But you still got the body. What the hell did you do with that?'

"And Hank says, 'Put it in my truck, took it up to Mendocino, and dumped it there.'

"'Mendocino? That's a long way,' says Ernie.

"'I had my reasons,' says Hank.

"After a while Ernie says, 'So I guess with that silencer, you got away with the perfect crime.'

"'Sure did,' says Hank. 'I sure did.'"

"After that Hank stumbled off his stool and staggered away, and I didn't hear nothing more."

Lenny performed another cigarette-lighting relay, recrossed his legs, and began tapping with the other foot. I sat in stunned and depressed silence. Becky, who must have found Hank's words excruciating, was also silent.

After a minute, I asked Lenny, "Would you be willing to tell the Marin County Sheriff what you just told me?"

He laughed. "See this?" He pointed to his forehead. An ugly red line ran up his skull into his explosion of kinky black hair. "Marin County Sheriff did this to me. So am I going to talk to them pigs? Yeah, sure. When hell freezes over."

I grimaced and let out a deep sigh. Great. We knew who had committed a murder. But we couldn't do anything about it.

As the phrase "up against a stone wall" echoed through my mind, Becky turned to Lenny and asked, "Would you be willing to tell Ray Alencar?"

That name again. The big-time criminal-defense attorney specializing in drug cases. The one the houseboaters had mentioned before.

But what possible use could Ray Alencar be in terms of bringing Hank to justice? He was a defense attorney, not a prosecutor. He had no ability to bring the power of the state down on Hank. Had Becky completely spaced out?

"Yeah, I'd tell him."

I thought again. Maybe putting all our evidence against Hank in front of Ray Alencar wasn't a totally ridiculous idea. Alencar was evidently a master of the criminal justice system. Maybe he could think of a way to get around Lenny's unwillingness. In any event, it was hard to see how a meeting with him could hurt.

"Fab," said Becky. "Let me find a phone and I'll call him right now." She started to get up.

I held her back. "Hold on. If you're expecting me to be at this meeting, don't you need to know my availability for the next few days? Tomorrow's intake day at Legal Aid, so I have to be in the office all day. The day after that, Thursday, I have a small trial in the afternoon, but I could meet in the morning."

Becky looked at me with exasperation. "I'm going to ask him if we can meet *tonight*."

"Tonight? Like . . . this evening?"

"Yes."

"Becky, it's almost seven. I can't believe he's open for new appointments at seven in the evening. Besides, I have to get home. My girlfriend's expecting me."

She tugged at my sleeve. "Could you excuse us for a minute," she said to Lenny. She pulled me up and away from the table.

When we were safely out of Lenny's earshot, she said, "Rick, I don't think you realize what a flake Lenny Rockman is. He's willing to talk to Ray Alencar now, but we can't be sure he'll to be willing to talk tomorrow or the day after. Or even be able to talk, given his drug consumption. We need to strike while the iron's hot."

"Okay, I see. . . . But does this mean driving all the way back to San Rafael?"

"No, no. Ray Alencar's in Bolinas."

"Bolinas! Are you talking about driving to Bolinas? Tonight?"

"That's where he lives and that's where he meets people."

"Becky, that'll take hours. And we might not even be able to find Bolinas."

Tourist-phobic Bolinas was notorious for constantly removing the sign along Highway 1 pointing to the only road leading into town.

"It's only an hour each way, and I'll drive. I know the turnoff."

Once again I felt myself sliding down a slippery slope. Oh Tiffany, Oh Tiffany, why couldn't I ever come home on time?

"Why don't you call Ray Alencar and see if he's even available," I said to Becky. "Maybe the whole issue of driving to Bolinas tonight is irrelevant."

"Okay," she said, departing for the No Name Bar's frayed pay phone. I remained standing where I was, preferring that to Lenny's cigarette smoke and twitches.

Maybe it didn't matter that Lenny wouldn't talk to law enforcement, I thought bleakly. With his emaciated frame, chain smoking, nervous tics and bad teeth — something else I'd noticed — he came across as the speed-freak poster child. Even if Becky and I were able to lure him to the Marin County Sheriff's Department, they'd just as likely arrest him as believe his barroom tale.

Five minutes later Becky returned. "He's willing to see us tonight. It really helped that I could say I was coming with my attorney."

"Okay. But I've got to talk to my girlfriend." Fortunately, by now we had a phone in our apartment.

My telephone call with Tiffany didn't go as smoothly as I'd hoped. "But I've already started working on dinner. Isn't this a little late to be telling me?"

Tiffany's response reawakened some of the guilt I'd felt after the infamous night on Becky's boat. But only some. This time, I felt, there was at least a moral purpose to my lateness.

"Tiff, I'm now certain Hank killed Kevin, and I'm pretty sure he was the one who tried to kill me. Tried to kill me, understand? I want to nail this guy, and right now we're inches close. I have to keep working on this, even if I get home really late."

Ten seconds of silence. Then, "Okay."

At 7:00, the three of us — Becky, Lenny and I — headed off to Bolinas.

30
RAY ALENCAR

Lenny, smoking and jiggling his feet, sat in the back seat of Becky's dusty, rattling, aged Chevy Nova. She and I sat in front. Becky was taciturn the whole way, understandably so. But I managed to extract a few bits of information. Yes, she knew Ray Alencar through Kevin and his pot-growing partners. Alencar was of Puerto Rican ancestry. And even if I resented my evening being hijacked, I'd at least have the opportunity to see one of the most far-out houses in Marin County.

After exiting Sausalito, we drove first through the jumble of Tam Junction. Then, leaving human habitation behind, we began to ascend through stands of redwood and oak, interspersed with patches of white-topped calla lilies. All the while I kept thinking, why am I creating another problem with Tiffany, in order to see Ray Alencar. He's a *defense* lawyer, not a prosecutor.

Topping the ridge, we sped through broad grasslands, the Pacific Ocean now in view, the setting sun in our faces. We skimmed past Muir Beach and Stinson Beach, edged around the Bolinas Lagoon, and finally arrived at the notorious unmarked turnoff. Without a moment's hesitation, Becky made the left turn.

Five minutes later, Bolinas, self-proclaimed capital of groovyness, appeared, architecturally a time capsule of the nineteenth century, culturally a remaining outpost of the hippie movement. Threading our way through crowds of dogs in the streets, we made several turns, finally arriving at a gravel driveway punched through a dense stand of pine trees.

As we turned into the driveway and passed through the line of trees, all the normal components of visual experience — land, buildings, vegetation — vanished. Instead, there existed only sky, sea and the sun.

The enormous, luminous sky — part pink, part grey and part all gradations of color in between — conjured a late Monet painting of infinite dimensions. The rippled sea mirrored the sky, except in a darker, more bluish hue. And the misty orange disk of the sun sat precisely atop the junction of sky and sea. I felt present at the Moment of Creation.

We parked and got out of the Nova. After an hour confined to the smoky interior of Becky's grungy vehicle, the fresh sea breeze came as an elixir.

We were perched, I now saw, at the edge of a rocky cliff elevated high above the Pacific Ocean. Along the cliff edge ran a lap pool finished in turquois tile. All was silent except for the distant sound of breaking waves. Despite having felt increasingly tense ever since Becky's call, I felt, for the moment, at peace.

I looked to the right. And gasped.

A flying saucer had landed next to us!

The spacecraft was about twelve feet tall, perhaps fifty in diameter, not exactly round, more like octagonal, white and smooth-surfaced except for a continuous band of softly-lit horizontal windows extending around its midsection. The disk appeared to float fifteen feet off the ground, but looking closer I realized it actually rested on a concrete center pillar, also white and roughly ten feet square

"What is that?" I asked Becky.

"Ray Alencar's house."

"That's Ray Alencar's house?"

"I told you it was far out."

Becky led us under the cantilevered disk to the concrete pillar. A pair of white elevator doors came into focus, and she pressed a button next to them. A security camera peered down on us from above. After thirty seconds, the elevator doors opened, and we entered an all-white space, blank except for another security camera. No one pressed a button — there was no button to press — but after a few seconds we began to ascend.

The doors opened to a well-fed man with a brown face and slicked-back black hair, wearing a white caftan with gold trim. "Becky!" he said spreading his arms. "I was so sorry to hear about Kevin. He was a wonderful person. I give you all my sympathy. You certainly didn't deserve this."

Becky fell into the man's arms and rested her head on his shoulder.

After Becky released, the man turned to Lenny, taking him by the shoulders. "Lenny, how are you? Actually, you don't look good. You must not be taking care of yourself. You need to chill out, man."

Lenny mumbled something and took out another cigarette.

Finally Becky introduced me. The man was, of course, Ray Alencar. "Good to meet you," he said, shaking my hand vigorously and looking me straight in the eyes.

"Come, everybody, sit down," he said, extending an arm.

I had time to look around the space. The interior of the floating disk had been divided in two, with the dividing wall running parallel to the cliff edge. We were in the front, ocean-facing half of the disk. The continuous band of horizontal windows I'd seen from the outside now provided an unobstructed, uninterrupted, one hundred eighty degree panoramic view of sea and sky.

Just at that moment, the sun was slipping below the horizon, changing from orange semicircle to pink glow. The sky was losing its pink patches but gaining patches of cream, while below the ocean shimmered, white waves against an indigo background. I shook my head in amazement. Hard to believe any one individual could have sole possession of a view this magnificent.

The interior of the flying saucer was sparsely furnished in High Modernist style — very European, lots of chrome, leather and glass. Oriental carpets covered the floor, and a faint scent of sandalwood perfumed the air. I sat down on a not-terribly-comfortable leather-and-chrome chair. In front of me I recognized a Barcelona table.

"What can I serve you?" Alencar asked. "Wine, beer, cocktails, coffee, water?"

"I could use some coffee," Becky said. "I need to drive back home tonight."

I too asked for coffee, and Lenny ordered a beer. Alencar disappeared for a moment into the back half of the disk.

When he returned, he and Becky exchanged happy memories of Kevin. The space in which we were sitting had apparently been the scene of some wild parties, and Kevin and Becky had apparently been regular attendees.

After about five minutes a striking young woman carrying a tray emerged from the back of the disk. Model-thin with long straight blond hair and pouty lips, she wore a dark blue cocktail dress and high heels. The tray bore two cups of coffee, a beer and a glass of wine.

"Thank you, Cybele," Alencar said as she served the drinks. Cybele then proceeded to light several candles scattered about the half-disk.

Preliminaries accomplished, Alencar turned to Becky. "You said you had something you wanted to discuss with me?"

Becky proceeded to lay out the case against Hank, starting with the disagreement over the small-boat harbor plan, Hank's performance at the membership meeting, and his attacking Kevin the next day. Alencar did not know Hank Foster and asked numerous questions. Where did he live? What did he do for a living?

Becky then had Lenny repeat the chilling conversation between Hank and Ernie Jordan. Alencar listened silently and attentively. With his full face, downcast eyes, broad nose and hands clasped in his lap, he looked like Buddha. Except Buddha never wore a white caftan with gold trim.

After Lenny finished, Alencar said, "I'll have to check this out. I think I can get hold of Ernie."

So Alencar knew Ernie Jordan, as well as Becky and Lenny. All members of the same secret society. Secret at least to me.

"If everything pans out, I'll deal with it. In any event, I'll get back to you." He turned from Becky to me. "And I'll get back to you too, Rick."

By now the panoramic view through the continuous band of windows had disappeared; sea and sky were dark. We'd completed our business and were all tired. We said our goodbyes, descended in the white elevator, and drove off.

As soon as we were off Alencar's property I asked Becky, "What did Alencar mean when he said, 'If everything pans out, I'll deal with it'?"

Becky dodged a dog in the road and made a right turn. She remained silent as she navigated her way out of Bolinas' confusing maze of roughly paved streets. I wondered whether she hadn't heard me, or simply didn't want to answer.

But once we on the road leading back to Highway 1, with the Bolinas Lagoon to our right, she said, "You asked what Ray mean when he said, 'I'll deal with it.' Here's my answer. Sometimes it's best not to ask too many questions."

Four days later, as I was returning to the office from doing some research at the County Law Library, my inbox contained a phone message that read, in its entirely: "Your theory was correct. Have taken care of problem. Good to meet you. Best wishes, Ray Alencar."

I crumpled the note in my hand. What did "Have taken care of problem" mean?

Then I heard an echo of Becky's dusky voice, "Sometimes it's best not to ask too many questions."

A week later, I received a call from Achille. This was unusual. In all the time I'd been doing legal work for the houseboat community, he'd only telephoned me once or twice before.

"Rick?" he said. "It's Achille." His voice was so weak and faint I could barely make out what he was saying.

"Hello, Achille. What can I do for you?"

"Rick, I fear something terrible has happened. I haven't seen Hank for over a week. He used to . . . ." Achille started coughing, a dry, hacking cough.

"He used to come and visit me every day. But now he hasn't come in over a week, hasn't even contacted me. I'm extremely worried. I've been asking everybody if they know where he is, but nobody seems to know anything. Rick, do you know what's happened to Hank?"

I took a few seconds to respond, at last saying, "No, I'm afraid I don't."

It wasn't a lie, totally. I didn't know exactly what had happened to Hank.

"Please Rick," Achille continued, his voice little more than a hoarse whisper, "if you do hear anything, get in touch with me as soon as possible. I feel so lonely without him. Hank is the only person . . ."

Achille couldn't finish the sentence. He was crying.

And for once, I felt sorry for the old guy.

31
GROUNDBREAKING

Three and a half years elapsed between Achille's telephone call and the groundbreaking for the Waldo Point Small-Boat Harbor. They were years full of incident — meetings with Strawberry Point Harbor Associates, meetings with the architects designing the new harbor, meetings with county planning staff and county counsel's office, meetings with the staffs of the San Francisco Bay Conservation and Development Commission and the State Lands Commission, hours spent pouring over maps and plans and making minute adjustments, hours going through the Supplemental Environmental Impact Report line-by-line and writing comments, and tense hours appearing before the Planning Commission and finally the Board of Supervisors.

To a degree that surprised me, the Waldo Point houseboat community pulled together and staged a massive volunteer effort. They sent emissaries to the Sausalito City Council, the Marin City Community Development Commission, the Marin Conservation League, the Audubon Society, the Save the Bay Association — *that* was a rough night — the Marin Housing Coalition, the Marin Tenant's League, the Grey Panthers, the Board of Realtors and the Building Industry Association. The county came to know the houseboaters; they came to know the county.

For me, those years were professionally rewarding. I was doing much more interesting work than the average lawyer my age, and I was able to see a cause for which I had recklessly stuck out my neck finally succeed, and succeed in a very public way.

But it was work. None of it had the searing intensity of those first seven months, starting with the visit of Becky, Kevin and Hank to my office on intake day and ending with Achille's telephone call. Those seven months I shall always remember. The rest, along with most of the other legal work I have done or will do over my career, will gradually slip away.

Luckily, the Saturday in November chosen for the groundbreaking turned out warm and sunny. Actually, the date was something of a fraud; we still didn't have the legal right to begin construction, as we were missing a needed permit from the Army Corps of Engineers. But the date had been chosen months in advance, and we were worried that if we postponed it, we'd be into the rainy season. So we went ahead.

The ceremony took place in the Waldo Point parking lot. Yes, once again, the Waldo Point parking lot. The community had dumped several inches of gravel on top of the dirt, and for once the area looked halfway respectable. Hundreds of people attended, not just residents of Waldo Point, but also people from other houseboat communities up and down the Richardson Bay waterfront, people from the Sausalito hills, government officials, supporters of the houseboat community from all over Marin County, and some who were simply curious. Cars ended up parking on the shoulders on both sides of Bridgeway.

I came with Tiffany, by now Mrs. Tiffany Spenser-Wong. She'd been to several houseboat parties over the previous three years and now felt at home at Waldo Point. In fact, Becky and several other houseboaters had attended our wedding.

That day Becky wore a fire-engine-red silk cheongsam with a high slit up the side. Stunning. She was going to be the center of attention, no matter how she dressed, so why not dress to the role? She looked as foxy as when I first set eyes on her, perhaps a tiny bit fuller in the face, a trace of fatigue around the eyes, but still radiant.

She was president and undisputed leader of the Waldo Point Co-op, successor organization to Save Our Waterfront. Her boyfriend was a handsome hunk, a bit younger than she, bursting with muscles and puppy-dog charm. He was a loyal member of the Waldo Point Co-op but played no leadership role.

My mind went back to the four who had been the leaders of the houseboat community when I first encountered it — Becky, Kevin, Hank and Achille. All three men were gone. Kevin, murdered. Hank, "disappeared," as they said in Latin America. Achille, dead of old age and a broken heart four months after the deaths of Kevin and Hank. The men had all fallen; the one woman had not only persevered, but triumphed.

Cliff Willis, the managing general partner of Strawberry Point Harbor Associates, and Lloyd Morgan, the partnership's attorney, were both there, smiling and genial. Originally I'd found Morgan impossible, but over the years we'd learned to work together.

Ray Alencar was not there, I noted. Had he been, I'm sure he would have encountered many people he knew.

The Co-op had erected a new stage for the ceremony. At its back stood a tall wooden billboard, topped by bold, multi-colored letters proclaiming "WALDO POINT SMALL-BOAT HARBOR." Below appeared an aerial view of what the harbor would ultimately look like, complete with docks and 110 houseboats, all painted in color and minute detail.

Three people spoke. Cliff Willis, the developer, offered a few nervous clichés and sat down after two minutes. Then came Becky.

Resplendent in red, she devoted most of her talk to thanking people and asking the audience to applaud. When at last she came to me, I raised one arm in salute and held Tiffany's hand with the other. As applause welled up from the crowd, I had to blink to hold back tears.

The final speaker was the county supervisor who represented the district in which Waldo Point was located. This was ironic. He was one of the last to come to our side, always fearful of taking a stand, lagging behind most of county staff and even several other supervisors. But we needed his continued support in order to access Community Development Block Grant funds, and therefore we needed to pamper him. He expected to be the principal speaker at any event he attended, and therefore he was the principal speaker at the Waldo Point Small-Boat Harbor groundbreaking.

He spent most of his speech praising himself for leading the fight to create the small-boat harbor and claiming that this was yet another example of his celebrated political courage. I almost gagged.

Once the supervisor had patted himself on the back enough, he, Becky and Willis moved to an area of specially prepared, easy-to-turn dirt, took up shiny new shovels, and uplifted a few symbolic clods. Ground was broken.

After that, refreshments came out, and people milled around and talked. The moment was so fair, everyone wanted to tarry.

One of the attendees was an activist with the League of Women Voters. She'd been of invaluable assistance to the houseboaters' cause, showing up at meeting after meeting, hearing after hearing, speaking whenever she could to endorse the proposed small-boat harbor, not only on behalf of herself but also on behalf of the league. She was an older woman, tall, with greying hair, wire rim spectacles and an old-fashioned way of dressing. Stylistically, she could hardly have been a greater contrast to the typical houseboater.

But I liked her because she contradicted the dominant narrative of the time, which was that everyone in Marin County was appallingly hedonistic and self-centered. This was, after all, the era of the sensational NBC documentary *I Want It All Now,* which depicted life in Marin County as all peacock feathers, nude hot-tub parties, and spoiled self-indulgence. This woman — Helen was her name — showed there was at least one exception.

I first noticed Helen that afternoon talking with Montse. Montse was speaking passionately and gesticulating with her arms, obviously making some sort of point. Helen was nodding — yes, yes, yes. Montse wore a Spanish-style black dress with red satin ruffles. As usual, necklaces glittered at her neck and bracelets jangled on her wrists.

When the two of them parted company, I went over to Helen, and we exchanged congratulations and thank-yous over the houseboaters' success.

Then Helen said, "I was just talking with Montse over there. She was saying the reason the houseboat community was able to win its battle and get the small-boat harbor approved was because they were so united. Everyone pulled together, there was no fighting or backbiting, it was all smooth and harmonious. She says that really the secret to the houseboat community's success is that it's like a big family, held together by love.

"I find that so inspiring. Is that the way you saw things?"

"Well, . . . " I said, stalling for time.

On the one hand, I didn't want to disillusion the good woman. After all, the truth about Kevin's death had never reached the newspapers. Few knew about the attack on me in the parking lot; few knew about Becky's and my sunset visit to Ray Alencar in Bolinas.

Plus, after Kevin and Hank's deaths, the community had pulled together and staged an effective political campaign. I was impressed.

On the other hand, Kevin was murdered by a fellow Waldo Point houseboater and SOW activist. The same houseboater tried to kill me. Shouldn't my response to Helen's question bear some relationship to the whole truth?

"Yes . . . ," I said hesitantly.

"And no . . . .

"And yes and no."

Acknowledgments

My novel shares its title with a documentary film by Marianne Dolan. Her Houseboat Wars focuses more on the southern part of the Richardson Bay waterfront—the area now known as Galilee Harbor—whereas mine focuses more on the northern part—Waldo Point. But her film is filled with images and narratives that capture the spirit, flamboyance and messiness of the era. I often used Marianne's film for inspiration and recommend it highly.

I want to thank my loyal band of readers—Leland Cheuk, Jane Cullinan, James Garland, Melissa Hurley and Kyle Roesler—each of whom offered valuable comments and criticisms and each of whom is a fine writer in her or his own right.

Finally, I again owe thanks to Gene Robinson of Moonshine Cove Publishing for having faith in me.